BETWEEN FALLING AND WALKING

BY
ARNO BOHLMEIJER

Contents © Arno Bohlmeijer, 2014.
Cover art: Wassily Kandinsky, *Blue Sky* (1940).

No part of this publication may be reproduced or copied, in print
or in any other form, except for the purposes of review and/or
criticism, without the publisher's prior written consent.

Published by Fruit Bruise Press,
an imprint of
Dog Horn Publishing
45 Monk Ings, Birstall, Batley WF17 9HU
United Kingdom
doghornpublishing.com

ISBN 978-1-907133-??-?

Cover design by
Brice Hendriks

Typesetting by
Jonathan Penton

UK Distribution: Central Books
99 Wallis Road, London, E9 5LN, United Kingdom
orders@centralbooks.com
Phone:+44 (0) 845 458 9911
Fax: +44 (0) 845 458 9912

Overseas Distribution: Printondemand-worldwide.com
9 Culley Court
Orton Southgate
Peterborough
PE2 6XD
Telephone: 01733 237867
Facsimile: 01733 234309
Email: info@printondemand-worldwide.com

First Edition published by Dog Horn Publishing, 2014

As an editor, I was immediately drawn to Dog Horn Publishing because of these six words:

books with bite. writing with risk.

Dog Horn has always been dedicated to working with writers with bold voices and writing that takes risks. When Fruit Bruise Press was created as an imprint to publish and publicise literary writing, we made sure to keep this at the forefront of our plans.

Arno Bohlmeijer is no exception to our one and only rule; this novel creates a space for readers to explore the places left in between. In between right and wrong, innocence and knowledge, and the realities which are stretched within families and culture.

Fruit Bruise Press strives to find the hidden voices, those willing to venture into unknown and less explored literary territory, and who are willing to challenge themselves and their readers with stories from the Other. Between Falling and Walking epitomises this whilst questioning business, family and social constructions and morals.

Alexa Radcliffe-Hart, Editor

BETWEEN FALLING AND WALKING

the biography of a prodigy
in 3d prose
by arno bohlmeijer

fearless and nearly painless:
a rare, dynamic, unlimited satire
on a shallowness as crazy as reality

With profound thanks to publisher Adam,
for picking this adventure for publication;
and to expert editor Lexi, for her keen and kind eye.

I

a situation of communication:
unheard of

'but try to love him all the more'
Sinead O'Connor

Fetched far

Losing the way, you may see a lot,
discerns a person who's making progress.
It creates blind faith, find they who've returned.
Sometimes I'm scarcely there and feel unbearably good.

This winter Jim is on the verge of superb independence while the river has risen to the levee top, and the other side is distant. As the Beaumond family have only recently bought a house here on the waterfront, Jim goes and explores almost everywhere, so Mum Helen is afraid that he'll slip away entirely: out of her life – especially in today's gale.

Bracing himself on the levee path, Jim is watching the gulls and gushing current, but no other mortals venture into the storm force. His sister, Romy, is listening to a Top Hundred or Thousand.

In the houses many lights are on already, although it's daytime, and plenty of televisions are on as well. Glancing in through a window, Jim can see some ski-jumping. *Mm, would be cool to float like that.*

There's a cottage that draws him specifically, because in the living-room with a colourful cloth sofa, loads of books and flowers, a music stand and romantic curtains, a girl his age is playing an easy and cheerful cello piece.

Next she picks up a painting in progress – an abstract full of deep hues – to work on it in beautiful concentration.

Still rocking to the contagious music, Jim rings the bell and is invited in by the girl called Allison, who offers him nibbles and drinks.

Maybe suspecting or pre-sensing something, she says after quite some time of soul and body enjoyment: 'Are you sure there's no need to call home?'

'Nah, told them I wouldn't go too far.'

About the truth and candour he's less awkward than the family's biographer, who'd prefer to skip certain episodes.

Faster than forecast, the storm has turned nasty. During this fierce rain and wind, Jim's mum is peering out a window through the vertical blinds. Even more concerned, she checks her watch and the large clock, squints out another window on the wrong side of the house and gets her phone.

Also prominent in the neatness of her mansion are a smooth sofa, a big mirror and considerable fitness equipment, reminiscent of American Beauty – the movie or more.

While the blinds tend to be ripped when a window is opened against logic judgement, Romy is lip-syncing a pop hit with a proper microphone instead of a hairbrush or carrot, shaking her hips and head.

Helen frowns, nearly drowned out by the gale and song, so she tells Romy to go and do homework. 'Any idea where Jim can be?'

'Up a tree by the water, waiting for lightning.'

As a funny little silence is followed by a dry clap of thunder, Helen curses the corny cheap irony.

'Just kidding,' Romy explains. 'Jim hasn't got enough of you yet.' And pleased, she eats a box of sweets that resemble life itself, or secrets lying ahead.

Among the roars and lashes of ludicrous or sarcastic weather, 'like biblical punishment,' Dad Richard comes in to throw an accusing look at his wife. 'What now: another Jim fix?'

'I haven't seen the freak for days,' Helen claims. 'The levee is breaking and you are so resigned, so given up, while I am worried!'

'Ah, worried to death about the head case?'

Richard makes a u-turn.

Furious at Rich or God and the dogged lost son, Helen drives around the area and gets out here and there, but her hair sticks to her cheek from sweat or tears, as the umbrella is broken too, used for pricking into the churning water with a fear to find their wayward son.

Over a mug of nice and old-fashioned hot chocolate in Allison's cottage, Jim peeks out, where the trees and fences are having a hard time. Although the young adults are in profound and frank love, their eyes are caught by a lone, plodding figure out there.

'My mother...'

'Oh...' Alli muses thoughtfully.

And there seems to be an extra gush or push of wind.

'You know, they want me to grow up and here I am.'

'Mm, trusting a stranger all alone in the house.'

'Are your parents out for long?' Jim asks.

'Yes. They're the best, full of confidence in me and my friends.'

'Justified! But I should be heading home, before my mum gets worked up.'

You see, in the forlorn past
we were walking to the river
and I never asked permission,
but it wasn't so deep anymore
and I wore my biggest booties.
Then I found the trapped horse
but there were swans and geese
and they would hit me really bad

so I've come home – don't be mad.

Treading quietly after looking in from outside, he takes the backdoor into the room, where a handful of neighbours and relatives are having a stiff drink, staring out. Sat on the sofa, Helen's face is buried in tissues and sleeves.

Jim swallows and shrinks into the gawking hush.

Chewing a salty snack and applauding from boredom, Romy studies herself in the mirror to train for public relations, re-arranging her hair. Richard's wise eyes have been travelling from his watch to the phone and back a few times.

'About this hurricane,' an aunt says with a glance at Helen, 'there are not enough casualties for the sponsored News yet, unless the levee... Anyway, the experts or government seem to *know* what they're talking about.'

Helen has moved to shake Jim and check his clothes. 'Where have you been? Are you smirking? Smack before these people who came to save you!'

Leaving the premises with a scare, a guest mumbles: 'Next time, Jimmy, your mum won't survive.'

'Nah, she *thrives* on this,' Romy says. 'Can I move out now?'

A devils dialogue
after this 'divine trip
with fine clean deceit':
'So where's the Light?'
'Oh, don't make no fuss,
I've been there, My Love –
just shut your f... small heart!'

View is the new film with true actors
and wonderful scenes that fuse too softly
since the Light crew went looking for Insight
in disguise, frightened that it might arrive unseen.

Within long Helen is watching her favourite show, *Oprah II or III*, and Jim is being stoical when Romy comes home to pose like a pro in challenging clothes and glamorous hair, adding a slick show dance to make Helen warily less callous.

'I'm practising for The Wise Girls! My band in a TV gig and ultra gig!'

'Hm,' says Jim, 'this new investor has faith in the case?'

'Yeah, *making* us!'

'To be trusted?'

'Sure, what's up!'

'I hate the trendy speak,' Helen says, filled with helpless contempt. 'I want a *new* child.'

'I wonder about Dad's input,' Jim mutters.

'But think of what's happened: my daughter kidnapped as a PR stunt for these Wise Girls, and my son running off with a mystery chick. What if I lose one of you? I do need fulfilment! Let's see how your dad is doing on TV, trying to earn the ransom back.'

In a stylish studio, Richard and the Oprah figure are proud in their armchairs around flowers on the classy coffee table, while royal music accompanies the crew finishing details. Already cheers and applause ring from the audience, until the hostess hushes them. One or two other reactions from the crowd are directed by assistants.

'Welcome live... our hero of the week... Mr. Richard Beaumond!'

And after some loudness of the crowd, here's one of the show's most spectacular openings ever: 'You paid and saved your girl's life...' (Rich nods nervously) 'from this beastly abductor...' (he nods modestly) 'and it *cost* you the last cent!'

An awesome lull is followed by a calm applause, as Richard drops the eyes, controlling himself.

'So how did you cope, handle, deal with it?'

He whispers to the camera: 'I prayed – to God.'

Bringing tears of inspiration to the audience.

'And you found like sort of, you know, I mean, your kind of inner being?'

'Sure, Love and Letting Go.'

Evoking spontaneous and emotional clapping, while reporters, crew and photographers are also in full fig and reverence when Richard and the Oprah descendent stand at attention beside the flags on poles, government-wise, with the prominence of their actions.

During majestic music the Second Lady offers Rich a big cheque, displaying it to each camera, their smiles and handshakes are turned towards the cameras instead of to each other, underlining the political weight and integrity of this programme.

For final footage she touches the reaching hands in front rows, until national traumas like an Olympic loss are forgiven or forgotten.

Steeper and steeper: fee of truth

For years I have suspected it:
this must be a crash course,
but no one says what for,
as the days are passing
and the Leader in me
does not stand firm
while by the hour
the odds will be
more costly –

Presently Helen finishes a bestseller about her Love & Suffering, translated in dozens of countries including Japan and Cambodia, says the literary agent in a press convention series. 'You won't believe what you read!'

BBC 3 is a co-producer of the film with introvert pervasiveness and an adaptation award: *Love & Lotto* becomes the great winner in Cannes, where Helen just gets overstrung from the buzz of it all. Her tongue doubles up in such a manner that a masseur calls it psychosomatic and a Reiki practitioner keeps the press at bay in vain.

Twice a day she asks Romy: 'What are you going?'

And to the agent she says: 'I'm all tensed upset.'

This results in a reality-show on BBC 4, doubling the book sales once more.

Romy is at a height of life where you may crash, because the ransom has been spent for many intents and media, and full of mirth like a musical chorus or cheerleaders bunch, the Wise Girls are poking auto-parodic fun at the secret source of Romy's fortune:

'A sugar-daddy?'

Romy laughs awkwardly. 'The Lottery.'

'The Robbery?'

'A legacy.'

'Hm, the mafia?'

'No, the sacrifices of my parents.'

'Ah, grateful for your safety?'

In their colourful and accessible dressing-room, all Girls are impeccable with costumes and accessories, stretch exercises and voice practice. Thanks to the scrupulous make-up and hair-styling, the Girls don't have too much individuality, except Romy, the recent financer and lead singer.

With pretty and synchronic dance steps, the three of them are talking to her like timeless and genuine friends.

'If your folks are that loaded, they can move to a better place.'

They add some Eurovision elements to their show-motion routine, and with tender courage or feeling, Romy embraces the pain of truth to open her heart to the outstanding and resounding magazine called High Life Style.

The concept grows into a serene musical called *Second Life*, as topical as timeless and universal:

The abductor lost his voice and the doctor said: "What have you *done* with it? There was even a deaf guy who could hear the foulness!"
He meditated and cleaned a lot of karma by refunding the money, except some expenses, and soon his voice returned, apart from some hoarseness.

In the Bible it's eye-for-eye,
happily invented by the Church,
otherwise the Pope had no Palace,
nor the billions to compensate abuse.

The powerful and profound musical becomes a whole of steps and sound, brimful of rhythm, passion and harmony with a chant-yell drive:

'Thousands of girls want a band like this,
it's posters, t-shirts and key-rings we need,
so people can *see* that we're here.'

University news:
the Soul is cancelled. Oh, it has served its goal,
but Feeling has been tough, so now it's time for Thoughts.
Will schools have any use for it – in Europe a book is published –
if the government grants a subsidy which used to be for music events?

Modest guide

Observing by itself
that words won't say
where an angel dwells,
the glory will keep quiet,
and whatever you've heard
is a presence of its own accord.

Alli's cello just fits into the car, next to a large bag with her dress.

The theatre, where Jim's never been, is a distinguished building in town. They take a side entrance and he asks if she comes here often, for rehearsals, but she's not very talkative.

'Nervous?'

Her nod is so sweet that he holds his tongue, and to what extent her concentration will be needed, doesn't dawn on him until they've reached the seats after passing a number of corridors. Jim has only seen this on television: a sea of velvet and gleam, flowers, and storeys of balconies.

'Here's your ticket,' she says. 'I'm joining the others in the dressing-rooms.'

He forgets to give her a kiss for good luck or success, he's standing there with the ticket for seat twelve in the seventh row, touching the fabric, then sitting as if these chairs are the seats of ethereal creatures, when the lights are dimmed and time stops to think.

The moment more people arrive, he notices the sharpness of his hearing again. He tries not to listen, but each voice and footstep is caught, while members of the orchestra take their spots on stage and begin to tune their instruments. It's unbelievable how free or fearless they appear to feel before an eager expectant crowd.

The house fills up with rustling and shining gowns. People read the programme leaflet, which Jim doesn't have, and now he's afraid to go and get a copy. Sometimes Alli's name is heard, and her photo is pointed at.

The last minutes bring whispering and squinting, before the director enters. He bows to the audience, turns around, lifts his arms in silence, and suddenly here's a spring of sparkling sounds, countless drops after days of thirst, all in such a strong surge that you move along inadvertently.

During a short interval the guests can stretch their legs and express a view of the music, have a drink and learn from the leaflet what's next.

Jim can *feel* what's next, but he doesn't realise it yet.

By the time his lips are dry and his hands tremble, there's a gasp from the whole audience, because the soloist seems to be smaller than her cello. She wears a long, corn-coloured dress, and that colour has the warmth of condensed sunlight.

After a little bow she sits down, the dress dropping softly, and people breathe in again, watching how the cello finds a firm hold. With a glance at the director, her face relaxes and the eyes close, she bends towards the strings, and when these are touched...

He doesn't even know what she's playing.

Soon he forgets it is human music; there is only a goldish glow.

After the applause, received by Alli gratefully and gracefully, the place will never be empty again. Jim doesn't want to move, but he needs to go and find her.

In the bustling dressing-room she's being kissed and hugged. A woman asks her questions and makes notes whilst her parents are on the side with the cello between them, where Jim joins them quietly.

The minute all reporters and organizers have left, Alli says: 'Pooh, get me out of this dress.'

Yeah, bloody fun!

Some games don't evoke a thing,
with their so hidden, dead-innocent depth,
which makes you bellow on time: enough already!

In tabloid land someone blabs that once upon a time there was a band called *Vice Birds*, and that Romy's group is feasting on the other success. The Internet is showing so much material of them that a piece on the cello concert is deleted.

Frenetic, the Wise Girls Promo Team launches some action on The Net and Television, and a law-suit against them has the obvious opposite effect: it makes terrific exposure. The entire nation is constantly online to follow this trial.

'It's over the top,' a newsreader adds cuelessly.

To be fired, and duly recruited by rivals.

What's the judge's fee in a court case like this?

Tempted by covert offers, he may remain sensible.

After extensive bargaining by awe-inspiring lawyers, the public pressure rises and the name *Wise Girls* can stay, which leads to champagne, a brand new PR campaign, tropic photo shoots and chronic jetlag, Security burn-outs, police overtime, bodyguard scandals, paparazzi calamities, fitness and de-stressing therapy per minute, mobs for the ninety-second interviews, Halls and Arenas sold out due to Celebrity bookings, Playboy sold out, vitamin or amphetamine programmes, limousines...

'No time for boyfriends,' shrieks a Weekly, 'but... ...'

Within a year they fill Stadiums and The Six O'clock News, with good back-up vocals because their voices have been affected by the media-training sessions.

Backstage a dark figure sneaks along a half-lit corridor, listening at a door, yet hiding in a corner for spooky footsteps with a shadow moving on the wall in silence.

Later this person tries another door and throws it open, camera focused, and already new headlines are hitting the twittering fans.

Man, it's time for a breather!

In spring Rich has taken up sailing in a distant marina, Helen grows dreamy and extremely inward, and Jim is happy, because they will not move house again after all, since the water line has dropped, and a lot of white and yellow flowers are blooming in the broad forelands. Most geese are leaving for the season, but gulls will stay and play and sway, now grey then deeply white in the sunlight on a dark sky.

Jim is often with Alli or on the track and field, where at long last his talents emerge, but today all Beaumonds are home, and Alli has brought her folks, to watch a widely announced Wise Girls show, worthy of their worldwide fashion brand that's reducing the Oscar and Bafta Red Carpets to useless.

Nice and cosy, Rich lights the fire place and switches the telly on.

'Channel 8, right?'

'Look, even The News has run long.'

'Louder, please,' Helen cries for the umpteenth time. 'Is it live? What's wrong with the mikes? Ooh, here are The Girls, it seems.'

Embarrassed, Rich turns the volume up again.

The lyrics may be lost, but in little tops with slipping straps – no bra's – for the close-ups and high-positioned sponsors – The Wise Girls are swinging their diet legs off.

Their performance is cleverly screen-split by footage of screaming kids all busy with flashing phone cams.

'Was the music live then?' Alli's dad inquires modestly.

'Yeah,' Romy explains, 'I couldn't even hear my own voice anymore.'

Which tends to spoil the healthy joy of it all.

Yet she does do her solo, and the high note goes so well that the Ministers of Culture and Economy give a standing ovation, to be followed by substantial subsidies.

The subsequent peace is nearly uneasy.

At this moment of delicate introspection, a log in the fire place breaks with such a loud crack that a shudder goes through them all, except Helen, and a sparkle at her feet that can set fire to the house is almost put out.

Extra item –
newsreader can't breathe

'Any idea where my voice can be?'
'Try TV9; do you have insurance?'
'No, they told me it would be safe.'
'So what on earth have you said?'
'Not much yet, really, except I...
misread the digits of dead people,
that were a bit lower than expected,
while the foreground tune was down.'

Wounded in wonder

And the land of milk & honey?
No, I couldn't care less about it
if it's closed seven times seven.
'Break open!' hears the cripple
and he walks onto deep water,
not very changed in the eyes
of those who don't believe.

Safely outside, if muddled and numbed, they stood and stared at Helen. The flames might have been extinguished, given the fact that the alarm was raised on time.

As minus multiplied by minus equals plus, Helen is utterly shaken awake by this drama, to tackle the long and ugly quarrels of the various Insurance Detectives very well indeed.

Fate is playing along smoothly: while the house is rebuilt thoroughly, after Helen's profound and very personal encounters with willing architects, Romy has gone on a world tour, Richard borrows a boat, and Jim lives with Alli.

None of them has a problem or asks where Helen is.

It's a year before she drops into a new mental state. As soon as the pond with a little bridge and living lilies as well as the drive and rose hedges are finished, the traditional blunders of contractors and workers fixed, requiring penetrating compensation, Helen is weeping again as if it's one of these post-natal depressions that she's always sneering at.

But she proves all the more how a weakness may bring out one's big strength, or even how they are really *one*: 'the new child in her life' becomes a priority for fulfilment.

'After Romy's and Jim's relentless rebellion, I'll go *pre*natal.'

However, Richard insists that 'one whacko in the house is enough, and *a son for soccer* wasn't much to ask, for God's sake'.

But burning with a faith that may need to reach further than she thought, Helen cries: 'This is something else! I can *feel* it, rising to a mysterious, groundbreaking, eye-catching occasion.'

'What about your age?'

'Man, don't be so gloomy! This film star is having twins and even Eastenders find something on the net.'

'Helen, that's the common masses!'

'Exactly.'

'And if it's Down-syndrome?'

'Shame on you, Richard; that would be removed on time!'

She sighs from impotence. 'Don't you know anything about medical science, these days, or don't you love me anymore?'

How lonely can one get? Helen wonders. Is her own husband the one to gather courage for something that will exclude her?

II

a singular light:
unseen

to consume the gift of love
with demands for perfection

New York Times Book Review

Sensible

Barks are a nice alarm clock,
howling makes you consider,
people's fear helps them run,
the poop doesn't discriminate
and the biting shows Feeling!

We'll take a dog after the baby.

The mental silence is taking baleful proportions. They don't need
jobs anymore; the book and film going public has been insanely
lucrative. Helen could write an equally successful sequel, *Made
It, Continued & Confidential*, the docu-novel about a parenting
council agency with an epidemic demand, but ideas are so
numerous that she doesn't know where to begin.

Romy is on tour around the globe, and each stadium is filled
with emotions which The Girls have grown immune to by now.
Jim has listened to his gym teacher: '...go sweat the trauma crap
out, because fibres and blood record or store more than you want
to know.'

And focusing ardently on athletics, he wins all the Regionals
already.

In a pre-Olympic locker room he's panting and perspiring on
the shower bench. Coach Maurice is calmly stern and handsome
in a heavily sponsored outfit. 'Jimmy, you've got speed as well
as technique, with power and dynamics; you'll have to *choose*
between track and field.'

Jim shakes his head and breathes in.

'Between running or jumping?' Maurice tries. To no avail.

And 'do what makes you happy' is all that Alli advises.

'Sorry, count me out,' Richard says after fierce new-baby
pleading from Helen.

'Oh, you're so selfish!' she cries, and she stands up abruptly to
stamp around and switch big lights on, as if that would make him
cave in. 'I'll take a good and sweet donor.'

'Yuck, poor soul.'

'Honey, what are you talking about? This baby will have an Oasis of Space and Peace here. Allison plays Bach or something in Vienna and Athens, Jim finds a kind of purpose as the hero of the field or star of the track. And me?'

She flops down again and raises the arms to heaven. 'This forsaken place is a graveyard, *craving* for new life. Love can't be stopped!'

Nevertheless, Rich remains mighty negative. 'You can't *do* that to a child. It will ask about its father.'

'Well,' Helen says very openly, 'you prefer an adoption kid from TV? So vulgar and impersonal! How to tell if its teeth are good?'

Helen calls Wilma Bishop, the astrologer who's known for eminence and integrity.

Wilma gives her a sense of trust or recognition, and a cross-section of Helen's heart and soul is on the old wooden table in a ranger's cabin without central heating.

There's sufficient firewood and Helen conquers her fear of fire; she finds the rural scents blended with coffee aroma rather charming, and gets into the right mood for a dialogue that will annul all materiality.

Between the coffee and slices of cake lies the sketch of lines 'read' by Wilma.

'That's it?' Helen asks genuinely disconcerted.

'All you need.'

'Oh, good. For a boy or a girl?'

As Wilma studies the sketch with full attention, a boldness unfolds in which Helen participates more than foreseen, about a past and future viewed so broadly that they're one basic whole, namely the spiritual world of which matter is merely a mirror – meaning sod-all to Helen. Physiologic this, pre-birth that, incarnating such and so...

As Wil does her job with skill and modesty, emotion and respect, Helen obtains insights of Cause and Effect.

'Implying Responsibility,' says a voice like Richard's in her head.

Which she never asked for and doesn't give a toss about.

She pays, aches for air-conditioning, gets a migraine and complains that she's clammed up – 'Any chances of a child down the drain!' – until by coincidence (something Wil doesn't even believe in) it appears that the Yellow Pages are just crawling with humanistic and *trans*personal astrologers.

Some of these also mention applied or relation horoscopes, career-planning and re-birthing, which confuses Helen while the clock is ticking expressly.

But later that turns out to be a lucky stroke, because she's cancelled The Pill only recently, and modern science reveals that prolonged use of the pill can damage reproductive cell tissue: ... *this prowling process leads to a decrease of the natural breeding powers.*

This also leads to Helen's feelings of haste, despite abundant modern alternatives.

Besides, in a serious religious journal at the hair salon she's read something about souls viewing the universe before conception. A soul is timeless and she knows about the survey of life one can get right before death, there are plenty of near-death examples on reality TV, but how can such a Christian or Buddhist truth feature in a Jewish story?

Although that does puzzle her, the baby urgency is only growing, and credulously she pricks an astrologer in the Yellow Pages, encouraged by the esoteric or plain symbolic fact that in the neighbouring country the book is universally called the *Golden Guide.*

This time it's a stylish, grave and intellectual man, who intensifies the event. In the end, over steaming tea in sunlight with crispy butter biscuits, Roger Van Der Vayne does tell her that she'll have another child.

He also mentions an issue like Ego versus Knowing, but Helen is so inspired already that she forgets to ask about hazards presumptive – for Insurance – and what the best moment for conception will be in which kind of Spa. Gratefully she pays in cash.

'Cosmic knowledge?' Richard stammers. 'With a bond of destiny?'

'Yes,' Helen speaks resolutely, 'or destination: I'll experience a deeper, interpersonal openness – like holy – of which many a measly mortal has no speck left! Oh bloody hell; he never said boy or girl.'

Heaven to earth

For a certain group
in the fast-stopping train,
this platform seems useless.
A voice on the loudspeaker:
'Between anger and grief,
Love will fall or walk!'
So can we change trains now, please?
'Attention, there will be one track
for Departure and Destination.'

Impassioned, Helen goes on the donor search as physical as spiritual.

One young man will be right, and on the west coast of Euromica – what a shame that the sun goes *down* here – she finds a clean and private resort where the costs are proportionate to the rates of taste, result and semen: the fresh donor candidates have to answer plenty of questions in a velvet folder, about the most profound matters like sizes and colours, IQ and star sign.

Due to the risk of inbreeding in the next generation, this clinic sticks to a *limited* number of conceptions per donor. It may seem only a minuscule chance that a half brother and sister of that kind will ever meet and breed, but life knows weird extremes, and given the supreme strength of these men's genes, it could be plausible that several offspring choose the same line of work or hobby, club or church unknowingly and get intimate.

To be on the safe side, Helen spends one of the handsome fire recompenses on a sizeable surcharge for the sole right of a donor with an extraordinary profile, who is fairly new here.

After taking great and brave steps, Helen is on a pretty candid ladies tour around the expectant and chic rooms of this renowned spa. As promised in the glossy brochure, the male host or guide is a famous role model.

On one door it says affirmatively: *Masturbatories*, in festive letters.

Inside there's nothing to hide either: wine and candles, light-classic music and expressionistic literature.

'In these most comfy and personal suites, for the most private product, you may take an excluding option for the donor of your choice, also to avoid social degradation.'

Shortly after the prosperous treatment, Helen leaves in a trance of joy and anticipation, although the many flight hours with stops and delays worry her: are these proper circumstances for the conception cells to settle solidly?

On the plane, when everybody is trivially watching a movie, Helen wonders: what's been set by karma already? A specialist journal at the baker's and doctor's talked about a diet that decides the sex of your baby, and quoted the causality insights of a film star at The Hilton: 'This horrible hurricane in China is a natural effect of their Tibet blemish and CO_2 mess.'

'Oh God,' Helen cries, 'was it *salty* for a tough boy and *sour* for a fabulous girl?'

Or is it all about the meat you eat?

'What if you get it wrong!' says the man next to her, who's been hearing a few things.

'Yes, the kid would be burdened for life!'

But after a moment of swallowing, Helen can see how silly she's been. 'When does a soul discover duality?'

'Well, the question is: when do you want to get pregnant?'

She laughs and pussyfoots. 'As soon as possible.'

The man smiles heartily too. 'The spiritual dimension is immense! It knows principles of pre-ordainment, and yet we make choices.'

Now Helen has so many new questions that she's struck dumb, almost like Zachary in the ancient story of disbelief. Come to think of it, was that also Jewish or Christian already, right before Jesus' birth and everything? Which religion would be compatible with esoteric astronomy? Or is it all universal? Where does a mortal belong? Is astrology as old as mankind?

Only after punishing Galileo in 1490, for saying that the earth turns around the sun, the Vatican got rather busy with the science of stars themselves. But later they failed to pray and prevent the Holocaust, or act against it.

'I think,' the neighbour continues, 'that a person's fluids texture is influenced by food. Male and female cells of eggs or semen must have their own "taste" and maybe you can lure or steer something or other with strong eating habits. But the thing is, how long in advance? Perhaps there's an Embryo Programme on the internet, for the desired sex?'

Back home, Helen tells Richard how much better this project was than the regular AI fuss of going to a shop where the assistant shows different syringes and asks: 'What size?' Or says without any affinity: 'Try them.'

In the best of wildlife movies
a whale is lovely and strikingly light
in very slow motion – from the safe side.

As if she understands and won't blame anyone,
a salmon Mum dies when it's her eggs that are safe,
before a bear or bird or person is on a fervent fishing trip.

Two weeks later, though, her period is distressingly punctual. It's
a big disappointment, but then she's given a choice all over and
can't help consulting her husband.

Who says: 'What's it to do with me?'

'Well, I'm only asking.'

'No, Hel, you ask too much.'

'But would you like a boy or a girl?'

'Now watch it.' Unintentionally he's begun sorting the baby
clothes that Helen bought on time. 'Next thing, you'll have triplets,
God forbid. They've got a sense of humour up there.'

'Oh, stop saying *they*; there *is* no plurality there,' she declares.
'Not even a *there*, you know, it's an omnipresence, a *Unity*, not
split into Good and Evil.'

Stereotypical, if doubting or desperate, she strokes her belly.

'And one God is behind all that?' Rich mocks.

'Not like a person, thickhead!' Helen is folding clothes with
superiority. 'It's the primal energy of love, the entire divine
spectrum! Think of the *bond* I have with this child as we speak.'

And her sweet look makes him shy.

She has a bite of cake and turns the telly on, landing straight
in athletics. This is less of a coincidence than she may think,
because Jim's popularity is rising by the day.

With cruel irony Helen finds that her cycle has never been more
regular. Instead of 'humour' she'd call it a 'work-to-rule' action, if
she knew to what purpose.

Briskly she books a full week in the Eurominican clinic, with the maximum claim credit, and on the third working day – by whimsical fate – she's running eye-to-eye into her daughter.

The office is a modern and spotless room with computers, neat and big photo folders on the tables, and on the walls are posters of gorgeous men and glorious pregnant women, slightly overwhelming to insecure clients.

Beside a shiny poster, Romy holds a pen and some forms in a cloth file with a golden string, filling them out in casual concentration, mumbling to herself and biting the pen between ticking off: 'Career... teeth and skin... size of this and that...'

She closes the folder and lays it on a table, to get a cheque from her bag, when Helen appears, deep in her own papers, looking up dreamily. 'Romy? Where do *you* come from?'

'How do you mean?'

'What are you *doing* here?'

'Same as you, I guess.'

'But darling, how old are you?! Which I know, obviously, so...'

'You don't, actually. It's close enough to eighteen, old enough for public relations. And you?'

'Hey, don't you have a concert to do or something?'

'Yeah, tonight, the Emperor Hall.'

They sit in the lounge and order a cocktail with tasty pastry containing a light advance hormone as good as legal, served in fine china by a highly civilized and fit young man, who retreats after an elegant little bow.

Helen wakes up rigorously. 'It's none of my business, I'm old-fashioned, don't worry about me meddling and baby-sitting, but what does your manager say?'

Romy is fidgeting with a colourful chocolate wrapper of a well-filled bonbon. 'We've been on the bloody road like shit-long, right? The *spirit* is freaking gone; been there and done it all twice! PR is bleeding to death, we're growing up, the Press are not keen on experience or maturity, and too many loonies are producing bands and screwing the stupid market! So Donald said kind of like you know... putting new life into us.'

She chews the chocolate.

'Rome, are you stoned?'

'Why?'

'I don't *know* you anymore.'

'So you take a new kid?'

'After what I've been through!'

'Well, for your information, it's my first time.'

'Exactly,' Helen says. 'Who's your pick?'

Romy takes a sip of something stiff and opens a fancy portfolio, pointing to an artistically hazy or steamy portrait. 'If you and me have the same guy, won't it be incest?'

'Let me think.' Helen changes chairs. 'You mean: our kids or the next generation?'

'I am the damn next. It's not as if we'll be sisters in law! Is it?'

Helen gets up nervously. 'Sorry, this is beyond me.'

And she calls the consultant.

His name is Fisher: a timid rookie. He and Helen and Romy are on the edges of chairs until he walks to the table and uses the computer that can show so many diagrams that something must be crystallised.

Helen points to Romy and herself. 'If our children have the same father and we are related already...'

Friendly, Fisher types and peers at the 3-dimotional screen. 'Excuse me.'

Perhaps he missed a solid basis in a foetal phase himself, and therefore even something normal may be a little menacing to him.

It's taking a spell.

'Stop wobbling,' Helen tells Romy. 'You won't get any dope here.'

And Fisher is ready for a statement. 'In your case the new generation, between second and third, would be no incest but pure and fresh blood, as it were.'

Like, needed urgently.

Helen sighs with relief and amends the sole-right claim.

Felled

Invisible, it is
lighter than ever,
if rather unknowing.

He can see and reach,
wants to *be*, but he's
not the right height.

Says a child about the
rustling that seemed infinite:
"It's not the trees that make wind!"

Helen has been so generous with her adventures in Euromica, that half the town suggests: 'Is Richard refraining from new babies because his gay phase is not latent anymore?'

And courageously he enters an identity crisis which, as one says in town, affirms a lot, and it makes the Press run hectically from one Beaumond to the next:

In a stilled mood of satisfaction, soberly smiling and bowing, Jim gets onto the rostrum, to receive a bunch of flowers wrapped in plastic, going with the gold medal.

His club (TBJ) organises more and more competitions, to be sponsored by bigger and bigger names towards the non-profit Games.

Despite herself, Helen watches the cheering and clapping audience during the medal ceremony in spotlights, with firework flashes of cameras. But halfway through the strong national song, Helen switches channels fanatically.

The office of Richard's counsellor has a brass name-plate on the door in flourishing letters. The male and very masculine Executive is taking notes at his desk. In a deep chair facing that,

Richard leans the elbows on his knees, head in the hands, then he braces himself to say: 'The Press are having a ball!'

Allison reaches the dressing room of a theatre where she's played the Dvorak concerto and moved the audience to tears with her gentle intensity.

She's wearing a gown of magnificent simplicity: straight, high neck, with a ribbon of the same sea-blue material in her hair.

A man in tuxedo brings her cello.

During applause in the distance, Jim comes running and hugging Allison, while the gallant man waits for her to take the cello and put it carefully in the case by the wall. When the assistant has withdrawn, she kicks her little shoes off.

'It was so beautiful,' Jim says, 'you were so good, the orchestra fell silent.'

With a ravishing laugh Alli turns her back to him, so he can unzip her dress, and she steps out of it, still wearing a supple satin slip, to drape the dress over a chair. From the seat she takes a newspaper opened at the sports page and points to a huge picture of Jim in action. 'You break all records!'

Quoting: 'Young Beaumond moves better and freer than athletes who've been drilled from early age, lost to the *joy* of sport.'

'So in a fucking way it's lucky that your parents ignored you.'

Jim tries to kiss her.

'Sorry, I need a shower first.'

'Me too!' and he undresses in a hurry.

In the prettiest writing there's a gold name-plate on the door of a TV8 office where the young, female and very feminine producer in a perfect business suit is composed behind her desk, handing a thick file to Rich, who sits and listens to her plea.

'Better than any other bidding Network, we can offer a Combi-Contract for all TV rights: two pregnancies with labour and birth, gay fatherhood, and Jim's Olympic Journey.'

So far that's been obstructed by both Jim and Rich; the first needs peace and quiet, the latter has *doubts* about his sexual nature.

Rich leafs and hesitates. 'Exclusive?'

'Of course.'

'24/7 recordings?'

'Yes, for a supreme price.'

'But what if something goes wrong during Helen's or Romy's labour?'

With a confident smile the producer reassures him: 'The viewers would learn and love.'

A multi-media offer for that package *plus* Romy-and-child's biography causes a complex tug-of-trust among the lawyers of all those involved, the case being that the Girls contracts have no clauses for the unborn and their rights, let alone for the options of a sperm donor with or without identity, presuming he knew what amounts were at stake (equivalent to the revenues of many ejaculations), and assuming that he parts with his semen for financial instead of emotional reasons in the order of an inferiority complex or this Compulsive Assertion Syndrome, which has been spreading like an aggressive virus.

A panic breaks out when Helen's second visit to Euromica turns out to have been 'a hit', as discrete sources put it, before the Sperm Spa signed a PR contract of their own.

A Yale scientist is doing research into the stress of foetuses, assisted by a postgraduate who specialises in the videography of the invisible. Helen is obtaining so much insight that her medical team can take a break, unlike Rich and his lawyers. Within days he reads a volume of gay EroSymboLiterature, which takes postgraduates a month or two.

'Why that shit?' asks a solicitor in her nobility outfit behind her silver name plate, reading the file that Rich got from the Oscar-winning documentary producer.

That sounds more flattering than the Golden Calf Award in Europe.

'Don't know,' Rich answers truthfully after some thinking. 'Maybe to re-group or re-orientate? Look at this piece; it could be me! Could it?'

'Let me see.'

'It's from Warren Leavitt's *Hidden Diary IX*.'

By courtesy of Random & Ransom.

* * *

After a long, frosty winter, the air is still crispy, in a titillating contrast with the sunshine. The sky is so blue that my yard has this pureness reminding me of early mornings in the mountains, turning into warmth and heat.

I take my jacket off and lean back, feeling the air on my arms, that haven't been touched for some time. Then it goes fast, can't help it: the shirt is off and a minute later the shoes and jeans are gone. Blond little hairs are tender on supple muscles.

I get up and stroll around, finding out where the flowers will come up. Walking barefoot in spring is like treading a desert island: it makes me feel powerful as well as vulnerable. The massage of my foot soles is sending new strength to the rest of my body.

This backyard is an oasis of seclusion, where birds and leaves can keep the peace. It's partly fenced off by trees and thick scrub, partly by an old brick wall, climbed only by a treasure of roses, bordering a cycling track.

I want to lie down, but the grass is still humid (it smells of yearning and promise and abundance), so I go into the house for a towel, near-naked in the coolness of the room, where a shiver runs down my spine. Still, I take my time, to relish the sunshine all the more.

Returning on the lawn, I spread a large towel and lie down on my back, to stretch until each spot of my skin is tight with delight. As my shorts are a bit wide, I can feel the wind going in, groping carefully. I roll over, the ground pressing gently against my genitals, and in order to feel that effect better, I lie spread-eagled.

Finally, when the sun is climbing, I take the shorts off. My skin is so untanned that the sun becomes a giant's eye and the wind is fairy's fingertips, finding a human being for the first time. They marvel at the down on my chest, which will soon be showing better on a tan, they tickle my nipples and shaved armpits, and then ride the muscles freely.

I'll stay this way and fade into eternity.

Which is a fate-daring wish. To be punished accordingly?

Much higher Self!

I've been wondering:
how can a form grow so
perfectly around the truth?

I'm bursting with modesty,
no room for more wisdom;
who are you taking me for?
I'm not fond of projections;
check your own mug head!

Romy has had a miscarriage and there's general relief, because
the lawsuits have become a web where a diadem spider gets lost.
Attorneys find shrinks who start practising fraud at the very sight
of the complications.

'Or is it called a stillborn?'

'Bad luck that she'll miss out on this TV contract.'

The News raises an exciting question: when is a child viable?
When is life worthwhile?

To avoid offence or vexation, they leave it open, but the issue
has drawn sufficient viewers to the network's website.

All contract offers are topped by those for Mourning Rights,
and before Romy can make up her mind and sign, she needs to
speak with Helen on a secured line in their Manager Donald's
office.

One Wise Girl chews gum, rubbing Donald's shoulders and
watching Romy critically. Expensively dressed, Don is broad
behind his desk, stroking a leg and throwing menacing looks at
Romy, who's tired, down-and-out, fighting tears.

'Oh, Romy, poor thing,' Helen says on the phone, 'I've seen
it on The Net. Everybody is talking about the funeral with that
plane-shaped coffin, the wings too big for a baby's grave. They
should have thought of that!'

'So, Mum...' Romy is forced to go on in doubting and harrowing distress, 'can we have your baby instead? Or else the Press Campaign is ruined.'

'But angel, how?'

Donald whispers into Romy's ear and she says, 'It's done here all the time: for the gay and barren.'

'I mean, how can you *ask*? Think of the *bond* I have with this kid. I'm *feeling* it. How can you be so egotistic?'

'But you *have* two kids.'

'Who are never around!'

'And what if you have twins? Could be the hormone cocktails we had.'

'No, sorry, Rome, you know how close twins are: when one of them is ill, the other will be too, even if it's in Stockholm or Bangkok.'

Jim and Alli are naked, lying on their sides on the soft carpet, caressing languidly and lovingly. It's very subtle: no sex now, just fingertip sensitive erotica.

With the lips light on her earlobe, Jim whispers: 'Where's your next gig?'

'Albert Hall.'

'Too bad. I'm off to Japan.'

And it's the Decathlon for sure?'

'Yes. The most complete of sports.'

'But the events are scarce. Which is also a good thing...'

'Wait and see,' says Jim, 'that will change!'

* * *

Just when I've lost all sense of time and space, there's a noise that throws me back into soberness: it's a motorbike, not in the distance like before, but droning closer and closer, not passing by but touring, circling, teasing...

Of course I should ignore it. *Un*challenged, the fun would soon be gone. I could go and check the mail, return messages or pour another coffee. But a drive of anger makes me jump into my jeans – never mind the shorts – and bolt through the door in the fence.

And it must be a break in my mind.

I guess I'm glaring at the machine like a crazy beast of prey. It stops dead in front of me, reined by a young man, looking back at me from his helmet.

'You, *moron!*' I shout.

There's no response.

'Take that stupid thing off!'

He understands my gesture.

At this instant, when his head appears, releasing a mass of curls around deep-light eyes, revealing both fear and defiance, I know I'm not my usual self: not quiet and polite at all!

Or am I discovering it right here and now: my true self?

He is silent.

Barely do I find my balance,
than *left* & *right* are abolished.
As soon as I've reached the top,
every level seems to be dropped.
So there's no middle of the road?
Honestly, I would not budge a toe!

'How brave of Romy to be on stage again, so soon and tragic,' say the public who are watching tonight's live show.

Helen doesn't even see the re-runs and debates; she decides to concentrate fully on carrying new life, because death and birth are such pillars of existence! There are documentaries with quizzes and games to prove their significance.

Being very pregnant, she's busy selecting maternity clothes in the luxuriant master bedroom, trying them on and watching herself in the mirror.

Aimless, next to a new pile of baby clothes, Richard is a stranger in his own room, with a mass-market paperback on his lap, reading it off and on.

'It's all in the stars anyway,' Rich mumbles as if time stopped ages ago.

'Yes, what's fixed and done so far... *Some*where it's been known forever, and yet,' Helen says, 'we still make choices.'

Pertinently she switches to the Discovery show with Special Guest, Stevens, a white-haired and very kind Unicef delegate, who is received with expectant applause, turning into awed silence when he speaks.

'Parents may pass on anything in the genes, but each child carries a uniqueness.'

The host is almost afraid to ask his next question. 'Why does one child take after the mother, and another after the father, and a third seems to be a misfit?'

Mr Stevens' answer is convincingly slow. 'Heredity, OK, but what a mean and painful and insane stroke of tough luck for one child with the sadness of Dad and this madness of Mum, hypothetically.'

A member of the Celebs Panel adds with startling authenticity: 'While the other is gorgeous and sporty.'

'Yes, there must be *more* to it than genes and chance, don't you think?'

There's edited appreciation in the audience, but Helen cries out: 'If a Soul is the Sculptor, and the Parents just offer the clay, who shapes the Soul? Uh?'

As if they've heard her, the applause is spontaneous. Can the crowd identify themselves?

Helen understands and she adjusts her diet: dumps all sweets, replaces sugar with calcium powder and malt syrup, and herbs can help against the hunger for 'something salty, savoury, spicy.' She also decides to eat unisolated carbohydrates and digestive minerals, doing so much yoga as well that she's barely getting to breathing out anymore.

Learning that a person or any creature is never *owned*, she sells a part of her assets and donates the takes to Amazon Children, the Lillian Fund, Foster Parents, SOS Children Villages, World Parents, War Child, UNICEF, Save the Street Kids, The Disabled Children, Foundation Hope for the Homeless. And she tells the attorney: 'Detach my TV rights from the Family Package. I'll manage.'

Jim enjoys each moment of cherished life as well, except once getting up early, when he seems to wake up before his body does, that's weirdly slow to get into motion, as if it's been asleep for sixteen years.

He feels reborn, the way a snake has a new skin, or smaller animals get a whole new body. That happens to insects until they're sexually mature, and then they get wings, which really reflects Jim's current state of body and soul. That sensation is primarily saved for Alli, but also for the training days on the track and field, where the eyes of bystanders blink, their mouths hang open and stopwatches are crushed in hands.

Thus he runs and clocks times that few people will ever know about.

At first he's wrapped in layers of clothes, when the night cold lingers in daylight. Taking them off in phases, listening to his muscles, he absorbs the warmth from inside and later on his skin, as a looseness grows in his limbs that's powerful: the paradox of an athlete.

That is not really trainable; it may only be recognised when it's there, to be fed with attention instead of power or stress. He can hear the sounds of nature and achieve a sense of streaming or floating.

With large willingness and some curiosity Rich is looking for something similar, even if it's uncertain at this stage of exploration whether anything needs to be discovered at all.

* * *

Weirdly unbalanced between wondering what I'm doing and knowing it only too well, I go on ordering him about. 'Get off, please.'

Without the helmet he looks disarming.

I move back to the door in my fence. 'Come here, please.'

After casting a glance over his shoulder, he pushes his heavy bike into my yard, then stands there like a schoolboy. Does he think I'm an undercover cop or something?

Instead of asking him questions, I close the gate and say, 'Take your clothes off,' as if this was carefully planned with a specific, educative purpose.

The absurd bluntness or sheer authority makes him obey without as much as a blink. Is he *enjoying* the crudeness? Pensively he takes off his trainers and socks, jeans, shirt and singlet, leaving a pair of white briefs, and for some reason I let him as yet.

There's enough to see anyway. I don't want to stare, I want to be casual like himself – that is, like his pose – but I forget everything else. So many details of that body are *begging* to be watched.

He's got the sizes and muscles of a man, the litheness and smoothness of youth. Which also reflects an inner conflict, I think. His feet are firm yet light on the grass, his legs apart, slightly restless. His arms are now akimbo, showing limber biceps, now leaning on his hips. There's no erection, but a great regular presence. Little hair on legs and torso, and only a whiff in the armpits. His skin reveals the finest veins in the slopes of his muscles.

I can't say how long we've been facing each other like this. Just as abruptly as before, I warn him, 'If you come and make that hell of a noise again, you'll have to leave without your clothes.'

There's no reaction.

'And now clear off.'

He gets dressed, giving me the opportunity to watch him at ease, to see every movement of his bright limbs, especially when he's standing on one leg to get into his jeans.

He climbs his iron horse and is gone.

I feel my penis against my own jeans, which I lower rather slowly, and when the wind spanks my nakedness, I'm embarrassed. Quickly I drop on my stomach. Will I be spotted and chased into sinfulness forever?

Shake free!

It's too sad, these moods,
like: what's happened to me?
Faith means: *have nothing left
but let be!* Or else you'll hate it.

There's not a soul who will say:
why the hell was *crying* created?

A few weeks before the expected date of birth, Helen's sugar level
is a bit high after all, not her diet's fault, and 'just in case' they
take her to the hospital, where something of consequence comes
up: breast feed contains important antidotes and a strong stuff
that's also used for doping in sports, but Helen is dreading the
physical misery of the feeding fuss. Romy and Jim were raised
without Mother's Milk, and look what they've accomplished – or
come to.
    'It's your choice,' the doctor says.
    Which irritates her terribly. Why isn't he saying 'your child'?
    Nevertheless she intends to offer it what she's got in her.
    As a preparation, to make the nipples grow supple and firm
already, she washes them with cold water without soap and
wears no bra anymore.
    Meanwhile she can often feel a little foot or knee moving,
making excellent footage. Actually the baby appears to be so
forceful and nimble, as the Network puts it politely, that Helen
must be all bruises inside.
    Well, she sighs to the baby, what have *you* been through?
    This can be shared with No One.
    I'm so scared to show the pain, she confides in silence.
    Hey, come on, that's what the viewers need!
    But what if I cramp and tear?
    Fine, they'll learn from it.
    Helen is not her usual self anymore. What kind of monster is
growing inside of her? She'd like to kick back, as a matter of fact,

if she weren't putting a strong face on it for the mass of viewing fans.

She gazes in the mirror.

Quite nice, basically, not the fat legs or swollen head that may come with pregnancy and her eyes have a gleam: the foresight of an exceptional child?

A cameraman is impressed and almost forgets to do his job. 'How are you?'

She dries her tears of sheer intensity and looks at him, this man with his fine face, unfortunately not the father of her child, and once more she needs to cry from something unknown, sliding into the arms that have held a camera for days, but the minute she feels his firm gentleness, she steps back responsibly. Which provides a shot to the director's liking.

Labour is way too fast; can it be that someone has accidentally switched syringes and given her no painkillers but contraction inducers? Was anybody in a hurry because the weekend begins? That should only happen in archaic rural novels: *village doctor is rushed off his feet between birth and death.*

However, Helen screams less than one sees in telly series; it's the baby who howls for two. Apparently the little boy is making sure that he won't be stuck with emotional traumas already: he gets them out of his system on time. And Doneus will be his name, rising to rare and singular occasions.

'Sounds like Donuts,' Romy grumbles on the phone in Vegas amid a trillion lights defying the recent energy and economy catastrophe.

'Damn, no,' Helen hisses, 'Doneus rhymes to Zeus! Is junk food all you're thinking of these days? This is Greek and symbolic, you know, or at least something of Latin origin. But OK, I'll call him Dono, just lively. Happy?'

The daughter is given a hard time, because Dono needs a breast feed and some nerve of Mum's is jammed there. As the whole birth mess went so fast that Rich is late and volunteers a causal connection, the phone is Helen's only outlet now.

She even embarrasses the reality TV director and producer. Anyway, these executives can always feed back to their ethical shows about ratings, where anything goes in order to discuss very openly the limits of admissibility.

Dono screams and squirms as if he's not angry but ill or damaged.

'Too much colostrum?' Helen frets, disillusioned.

'Can't be,' says the doctor who was in favour of home labour.

Are my nipples too flat? Helen wonders privately. I should've had them done before!

She's wincing with the after pains, but that's nothing compared to the infant's convulsions.

'What the hell is going on?' Jim asks, returning from a training session, sweating less than his mother and baby brother.

'This little person is either disturbed,' the Nanny observes, 'or highly gifted.'

'How can you tell?'

'Wait and see.'

It sounds definite enough for Helen to take a close look at Jim. In which category is he?

And telepathically he asks: 'Was I that mad too?'

Helen's tongue dries up. 'Can't remember.'

It must have been repressed like the worst rest of life.

Before Jim is risking an insight of regression, shedding more light on his mother, he takes to his heels, and Helen stays behind in a contemplative state of mind. What is Jim's and Dono's common denominator? That would or should correspond with her genes. Must be genius rather than defects.

What a good change to do some *thinking* for a minute instead of feeling. Those who say that it's outdated are just not capable of it anymore. The States have now 'found out' that China knew about the two brain halves a thousand years ago.

So why did the Chinese economy take so long to bloom?

Let's see if I get this right: is *yin* almost helpless without *yang*?

Yes, despite the brilliance of one half.

And Helen does feel better.

Until Dono needs the breast again.

Can she quickly ask for a little sedation? If that medication reaches his blood via her milk, it will do him good as well!

Nanny lays his belly against Helen's, mother and son on their sides with cushions in their backs, and Nanny says: 'A healthy baby inherits natural reflexes. Oh! Sorry, I didn't mean it that way.'

But it's just as if he gets the message. His tiny chin touches the softness of her breast; his whole body and soul are sucking. With a shiver Helen discovers that this creature is both brittle and magnificent, able, ageless. What a task for her to be raising him! She suddenly knows how far it goes.

***

Satan must be waiting to clasp me in his claws, but rolling on my privates, with the sun on my bum and back, I'm panting with pleasure, and when a cloud moves black before the sun, I can just grin at the coincidence, which may be as symbolic as it likes! Where's the wrong I did? There's been no fight, no force. What fear did he show? It's not his fear I enjoyed! Even if there *was* any apprehension, my anger seemed justified, since all I wanted in the first place, was to put an end to that infernal noise. Although secondly...

When the sun is back, it's fiercer. I turn over and stretch, exposing every spot of flesh.

I do check the mail and return calls, try some painting in vain, buy groceries, and cook a meal. Yet that body keeps blocking my sight and mind, gleaming not with sweat but with health and strength. Above all, the emotion in his eyes is touching me over and over.

I can't sleep very well, but the morning is fairly normal. I'm looking forward to another day outdoors.

It's almost noon and soon enough I'm lost in this bliss again: it's still here, all-pervading. So when a droning sound comes closer, I already *know*. It's the same hovering and howling. Don't listen, man, don't pay any attention!

Let's not turn this into a battle; he's come back and whether it's evil or playful or a question, begging me to respond and solve something for him... Never mind!

Wearing swim trunks I go cautiously along the shrubs, tickled by leaves and twigs. On the edge of the open I stand and lift my hand. He can dodge me easily across a patch of grass, but he stops, takes his helmet off and catches his breath. Without a word I turn back.

Universal belief in me

What a perk of adversity:
to turn it into more poetry
that will always be quoted,
provided it's nicely cryptic
and rising above Daily Life,
otherwise it would be tough
on those who are recognised.

When Jim is unsettled and losing his rhythm, which rarely occurred before Dono's birth or the need to evade reporters on the field, he may even blow the 400m, his favourite discipline. Then he fidgets with laces and makes a false start, the headwind annoys him, and the bends are a pain.

'Hey, man in form,' a photographer shouts, 'go home!'

And the paper will say: PRECOCIOUS TURNS PECULIAR.

It's no use going home, where Dono is restless again and a producer calls him 'Oh No!', although the commotion attracts more viewers again.

'Prick,' Helen defends her baby, 'it's only his tummy. I've just had too much garlic.'

She can hardly change his name once more; that would add an identity problem.

The more crews are overwrought and leave without replacement, the calmer and quieter Dono becomes.

'Little smart ass,' Helen says a bit ashamed and afraid of the future. But he's bound to react to fear, there's nothing strange about that, so she contains herself.

Like Richard, Jim and Alli move to rooms in another wing of the mansion, grateful for the detachment of TV contracts, and they can keep some distance from circumstances that are not their responsibility.

When Jim's passion for the decathlon hits the social media, he's told that the specialist scores are much more spectacular, but he won't restrict to one discipline day in day out: 'Boring and unhealthy.'

At one of Alli's concerts, a rare awareness grows in a corner of Jim's being, to transform itself on the track and field: sounds and rhythms in his muscles. Manifested in motion, they take the public's breath away.

What Dono feels in his body remains a mystery too. The squirming and screaming may have mellowed, but the energy is still such that he needs to be tied to the mattress in order to prevent accidents.

At the age of eleven months, he's found standing up in his cot with the mattress on his back.

'Hey, little Samson!' says Helen. 'Will you be that special? Better be careful, you know.'

All this time she's been trying to get used to him so hard (for years she'll tremble at the sight of her doctor or when any baby cries) that she's not even surprised anymore. After making herself decent with the help of modern cosmetics, Helen walks up to Dono and gapes into his big deep eyes.

'I'd swear he sees more than us.'

'Or more than we!' Nanny suggests.

The mattress is tied solidly to the bottom of the cot, and Helen realises how badly she needs a deserved break.

It brings her to Paris, where The Wise Girls are recording an album. Normally such business leaves no time for a chat with your mum, but the current mental coach says that Romy has to reconnect.

The Marketing team agree immediately, because one of the Girls, Lisa, nearly got out of life altogether, as the insiders know. For which tabloid will they break the radio silence as soon as Marketing & PR can profit from that?

Romy is said to have odd moods, a hormonal effect of 'the baby phase', which undermine the publicity codes. All of a sudden she's having moral problems with a TV interview when the questions and answers and gestures are discussed beforehand.

In this foreign studio the Wise Girls with Donald and the Crew, Host and Make-up hands are rushed by the producer. Despite their fame there's no escaping the Producer's voice: 'Thirty seconds!'

Grimly Donald speaks to each of The Girls in turns –

'Remember: be timidly candid.

Be shyly intimate and strong.

No trace of struggle or disharmony!

OK, there you go!'

And at the last second he hisses to the excited host: 'No surprises!'

They're on, in a close buddy row, after few rehearsals.

'Do you ever cry?' is one of the first questions.

'Yes.' (Timidly candid)

'When was the last time?'

'Um... When Lisa left the band.'

The way she holds her tears, conveying no trace of disharmony in the group, is rewarded by warm applause.

'What's the favourite part of your body?'

Quasi caught off guard: 'Oh... my...n...'

'And they're always erect?' Over speculating squeals – 'Has she actually said it?' – the host gives a cute wink on camera, to be followed by a hush. 'You did say nipples!'

Shyly intimate and strong: 'This isn't in the script! Oh...'

Girl Two looks around guiltily, self-consciously, giving away the insiders fact.

And in all confusion the host mutters: 'Can we see?'

Mettlesome and benevolent, they improvise a young-among-young gesture with quickly visible nipples. After all, a boy band did that ages ago and got away with it even in The States.

The applause full of playful or appalled cheering and drumming is edited again, because the selected crowd were quiet from emotions like uncertainty. Many a cheek is fiery red with the fear of censorship. Everybody knows how Playgirl TV was punished over something exposing itself too spontaneously.

Sauntering by the river Seine in twilight, disguised as regular people, Helen and Romy watch the touring boats with their happy lanterns, laughter and dance music. The water is lapping the quay confidentially, floodlit buildings are reflected imposingly, the antique and romantic strings of lamps cast a stately light on the trees, for which they have little attention; maybe they're called sycamores or anything else.

It's been long since they walked in daily life.

With a Vogue rucksack, Helen sits on a bench where Romy comes in tears, wearing a cap and dark glasses, but not the same as years ago for painfully different reasons, when the abduction was staged so realistically that it was a hype success in which even The Girls believed themselves.

'Isn't this nice and bohemian?' Helen says.

While she pours tea from a thermos, and offers ordinary biscuits, neatly enjoyed by herself as well, Romy flops down beside her, mumbling uneasily: 'The best food ever.'

'Except like in the old days?' her mum says.

'Can't remember. I grew up so fast.'

'Yes, and my Dono is even quicker. The other day somebody said quite rightly that he's turning into a real person.'

'Lovely,' Romy says.

'Thrilling, isn't it, this wooden bench in the open.' And Helen laughs about her own wit: 'Leather wouldn't work here, right?'

'Yes.'

'So it saves the lives of a buffalo or two.'

'Does it?'

'Hey, are you high again or something?'

'Just a bit sad, I guess.'

'I understand. About this Lisa who left?'

'Hm.'

'Haven't you heard from her anymore?'

'Nah, she's busy writing memoirs.'

'Ah,' Helen says, 'throwing dirt on everyone.'

'Look, a black and a white swan.'

'Yeah, pretty.'

'And rare, I think,' Romy says with a little shiver.

'Sort of royal, actually.'

Their eyes follow the pair's unruffling water strides until they're silhouettes.

'Are they really that proud?' Romy asks eventually. 'Or is it just the way they look?'

'Well, truly proud, I'd say, because the way you look, says a lot about one's inside.'

And she flicks her lank hair.

Romy is momentarily sagging a bit. 'Will they have grey chicks?'

'Can't say. Would be special though. Dono is just blond.'

'Oh.'

'Handsome little bloke, and you know, if you have kids, he'll be an uncle already! Is that correct?'

Romy is silent.

'But don't make them call him Uncle. On the other hand, that would be awfully funny, don't you think?'

Romy chews a piece of bread that seems to be stubborn and, sagging some more, she says: 'I don't think the band will survive. Unless we'll serve as a computer game or an online clothes label, you know, kind of like Fine Design Nine.'

Helen tries to put an arm around her empathically. 'So you're afraid to be redundant next?'

Romy shrugs. 'Are you nuts? I just want a break! As the lead singer I'm always in the front, right, and we don't have days off like normal people, do we! When the other girls fall asleep or pass out, who cares; the tapes and dancers will fill the blanks.'

'Or the 3D big screen and firework lights.'

'But for me...'

Discretely Helen pulls her arm back. 'Why don't you cut down on concerts? You don't need two a day, between the photo shoots and interviews.'

Romy starts crying hard. A whole day off... It becomes a mental catharsis which their corporate psychologist couldn't dream about, and her awareness of reality is all the more cruel. 'We've signed up; we've hired new stylists, the best and most expensive.'

Helen is almost emotional too. 'You're a grown-up girl, Rome, it's what you always wanted, and I've got a baby to care for now.'

In full spirit she pulls herself together, chucks the thermos back into the rucksack and is plucky enough to take a taxi to Gatwick for a very-last-minute flight, beginning a round trip with a variety of improvised and surprisingly extendable stops, denying the world crises.

***

Why does no one else protest in this quiet area? They must be thinking: don't heed him, don't feed his need of attention!

I'll give it.

His helmet is off and his hair is all wild. How I'd like to run my fingers through that, massaging the skin. And I think he can read my mind; with a shyly triumphant smile, he wipes a shock of hair from his brow. This takes me by surprise for the very reason that it reminds me of the threat I made yesterday, but simultaneously that same directness and determination return.

'This way, please.'

He follows me through.

Walking into the light of the lawn and sitting down in the deckchair, I'm pleasantly awkward, while he's stopped in the same spot as yesterday. I put my arms behind my head and say, 'Undress.'

By accident he fails to lower the zip of his jeans all the way, so the shorts go down a bit as well. In a reflex of politeness or faintness I shut my eyes.

When they're open again, he's lifting the shorts back over his thighs, and stepping out of the jeans. How lithe those legs and feet are, how natural on the grass.

'Off.' I point to his shorts.

He slips them down again.

He's totally, stunningly naked.

Innocently?

'Out.' I point to the gate, out of my mind.

He walks erect, at a normal pace, smoothly like a model with more talent than experience.

The hard spot was long ago,
I've started all over and again –
I believe this to be my seventh life,
so give me the time from Now to Ever
for a durable unison of Courage and Luck.

Bumps can be jumped, but I flunked each class.
Life can be a dice, and who is always rolling twice:
this bully from class Twenty or so. Hey, wait a minute,
my dice becomes round and crystal... It's hitting bull's eye
in a place that looks reachable. One day I'll be in the Right Year!

Quite matured, wearing phone and music plugs (aged two or three
now?), Dono is in the middle of the room, building something
elaborate with wooden blocks.

Also wearing earplugs, a camera woman is bored in a corner
with not-so-light drinks, checking the cam with one hand, gaming
with the other, watching stubborn re-runs of the Old & Beautiful.

Dono must be three, with techno parts in his big-boy bed
numbered up to a hundred, and he's trying to pile them in the
right order – is he? – while the woman is asleep on the floor.

For a moment, returning from Berlin and Singapore, Helen
stops to watch him with a tragic headshake, then she walks on to
the stairs.

With a leap of instinct, Dono flings a block after her, and the
cam woman is all zealous again.

Untouched, Helen enters Jim's flat, who'd share the care of his
baby brother with Richard, and she finds him and Alli in a king-
size bed.

'Where did you get that?'
'It's a gift from sponsors.'
'Oh, including condoms?'
'Mum, I'm eighteen!'
Helen ponders.
'Alli... you must have another concert or something coming up.

Don't follow the example of your sister-in-law; she's lying on an old bench like a tramp! My youngest seems to have the soundest mind, unlike my husband with his "literature", addicted like an adolescent.'

What a blessing that she's got a part of the house to herself.

But a mad sort of nostalgia creeps upon her, especially after the recent scene in Jim's room, of which the harmony was rather shocking.

The doorbell rings and Dono flies to get it, but Helen storms after him and snaps: 'Go to your dad, I mean...'

Confused by her mistake, she opens the door, pre-occupied.

A very friendly and handsomely groomed man in his thirties introduces himself: 'My name is Roy Milton. Is Mr. Beaumond in?'

'Are you the Network Lawyer?'

'Um, as you wish. Mr. Beaumond is expecting me.'

Dono tumbles across the large hall and his movements resemble *martial arts.*

'Oh,' Helen says, 'I suppose my husband hasn't heard the bell; we've done an extension. Come through and don't trip over the kid, even if it isn't his.'

'Oh, *my* coordination is alright.'

Dono does an intricate yoga thing and Roy points to him. 'Is he a dyslexic?'

'No, an *eclectic!*'

Hm, runs in the family?

And quickly she adds: 'He doesn't like toys, that's all. Doesn't see the use of them. The stupid stuff is everywhere, so he can't walk without stumbling, and silly cynics will say it's ADHD or something. In the old days it was called MBD and at least you *knew* what you were up against.'

'Perhaps his *nerves* are disturbed. How come? I wonder, in this peace and quiet.'

While Dono does a Wise Girls act, Helen hurries to the new wing door, saying, 'When he's after sweets, he can walk perfectly straight!'

Roy says in the doorway: 'Look at him now, doing tai-chi in the Dalai fashion?'

'Yes, half of Hollywood is Buddhist already.'

So Helen is positive: Dono is *not* rightly seeking attention.

'Missing his daddy?' Roy calls over his shoulder.

Dono pauses in a thinking pose and Helen's eyes go blank. She closes the door behind Roy and stays there listening, but Dono is frowning, so she rushes up and puts him behind the computer.

While he's going at it as if he knows what he's doing, Helen plants herself by the life-size mirror on the thick soft rug, where she used to lie naked and dream away, caressing and forgetting. She pushes her breasts up, considers a procedure without a big risk of cancer, and makeshifts a new hairstyle with a half-long natural wave, for a change, wiping wrinkles away that are caused by a smile, still observed wondrously and critically by the kid.

Bravely facing a message

Unexpectedly I get a dream
which really describes it all,
but it requires an explanation
and strives to be true as well.
OK, I'll work on it big time,
as long as they won't push
and make me go too deep.

Jim not only wins Design furniture, also money, major medals, country-side trips, and a motorbike that's drawing shy attention from Rich, who'd like to try it someday.

What the youngsters were celebrating the other night is the news that Alli can change her Beijing scholarship, won at the Inter Asian Competition, for a domestic Master Year. Her request has caused a bigger rigmarole than the competition itself, which she attended in her usual way: modest, free, and enthusiastic.

Given the joy she derives from life and studies, the fatigue that comes at some point is almost a paradox.

Jim's experiences on the track and field are similar, and their fulfilments mingle tenderly. Returning from intense and demanding trips, they nestle together, tasting and feeling with the eyes closed from delight. Their skin and muscles relax to the utmost.

After a long shower, the lightest of touches bring about so much, that each pore is a sense, and then comes the urge with pauses and drives, in a surge of strength that begs for a full fusion, when receiving is also giving.

Helen feels terribly wistful again. They're so young, their bodies mighty tight and smooth!

She curses a crew straying in the garden, where Dono has grabbed a camera – this crooked kind of footage brings in Emmy Awards actually – and his 'straightforwardness' drives them crazy too: 'Like a butterfly, the prodigal toddler is never at one activity for long, he always trips and drivels, breaking things or babbling in his own way: indistinct and incessant.'

If he does miss a dad after all, the ungrateful wayward brat, how the hell can she be two parents?

Reckoning that Rich will romp and play with him occasionally, she invites him over comradely. 'Have a nice muffin. I've made nostalgic good coffee, let's be honest: it's been ages. You can really come and watch television here, you know; we'll have Jim and Alli too, Do will dribble so cutely at our feet. Why don't you give him a football? Have you been to that Sports Arena of Jimmy's yet? And Romy misses you as well. I can confess that...'

She can't finish, getting very busy with the coffee and heavy special treat.

Richard has cleared his throat self-consciously, to say: 'Helly, I've changed so much...'

'Me too! But *you* don't communicate. You've got no idea of the transformation around here.'

'I mean,' he goes on vulnerably, 'I'm returning to school.'

'To do what?'

'Cultural Androlosophy.'

Dono seems intrigued.

'But what about Life itself?'

'I'll *find* it there, enlarged and enlightening.'

'*Blinding*, you mean. Life and Art and Science are found on the street!'

'Yes,' he says kind-heartedly, 'to be described and saved.'

'No, that's an Escape!'

Melting, Helen looks at Dono optimistically. In a gallop he rides his large-or-real-as-life rocking horse, the heavenly eyes on Rich, who withdraws modestly, then he rides too hard and topples as if they were part of a farce. Helen turns away in dismay, but all intact, Dono follows Rich and on his way he hits the computer keys, after which something exceptional appears on the screen.

Helen consults the Yellow Pages again and calls a Special School. 'Ah, thank you... No, that's my other son. And um...' She casts a forbidden glance at the TV camera. 'Excuse me, do you take a preconscious, I mean precocious pupil? ... Yes, five days a week, please, by taxi.'

In even higher spirits she waves to Dono, who types melancholically.

Each morning at the expensive institute he cries heartrendingly, but Helen trusts the reassurance of a teacher who states: 'They often cry as long as the Mum or Dad is here, which will definitely be over, provided no depression or mental condition runs in the family, like an illness of the soul or a psychic disease?'

'No, only the psychic high-sensitivity.'

'Oh, there's medication for that, right? Ritalin, twice a day.'

'And side-effects?'

'Trust me, you don't want to know; it would only make you autistic.'

***

What have I done!

I jump and run, feeling like crying and laughing.

I'll take it all back and explain!

What then?

That manly young nakedness, walking away, has struck me dumb.

From the gate I'm watching the shades of branches on his bare back and buttocks, until he's reached the motorbike. He throws a leg over it, starts the engine without any effort – his foot so slender on the pedal – and he leaves with an open look over the slope of his shoulder.

It's always been a cliché dream to ride a horse naked, but this... What the hell does he think he's doing? Taking me *seriously*?

Back in the yard I pick up his clothes with the fragrance of his nonchalance, brushing them against my cheek and chest, and I put them on, tasting the ironed cotton fibre: it's an aching after long privation, making me weak.

If the police find him, will he turn me in? Then what: deny everything? Act a brotherly friendship and practical joke?

My doorbell rings.

It's a scary agreeable feeling to answer in the stranger's clothes.

'Kirsty! Hi...'

'Can I come in?' one of my best friends asks with a jesting, hurt smile.

I think of the helmet lying in the yard. 'No, sorry.'

She laughs, moving forward and assuming that this is my funny way of criticizing her politeness, but I stay put with my brand new and killing candour.

She stops dead. 'Oh. Bad moment?'

I nod, looking at her as neutrally as possible.

'OK. I love you anyway, and I'm so glad you're not apologising! But I hate you today.'

While she gives me a kiss and turns back, I can hear a certain motorbike coming closer at a slow pace. I'll recognize that 'hum' for the rest of my life.

Warm hoarfrost

or it's a reflection
of the first sun ever
and a moon that stays,
as the swans there know;
they'll lift their own weight
with those who also understand,
for a sublime flight over water and land.

It's early in the summer and early on a lovely Saturday, four and a half years after Dono's birth. The break of day is so deeply peaceful that it wakes Helen. She swathes herself in her robe, still relishing the sleepiness: you needn't do anything today, just drink a sweet cup of tea and choose: huddle up all snug in bed again or do a bit of work after all for extra satisfaction?

She's been rather fond of cleaning recently, and that is already done this week. Reading to Dono is no option yet, because he's comfy and quiet in bed. A work-out, some gardening, fine arts? Nothing is really necessary now. Write a brisk book about motherhood? Nobody does that!

Make a good breakfast for everybody?

Musing along, Helen can see how wonderful it is outside.

She opens a window and lets the air in – mm, the scents and songs... What a pity that those crows are always dominant; they often make her close the window.

The forelands are still dawn hazy, yet it's also light – with moon or sunshine?

Is the source of everything invisible?

The ground mist is so dense, the cows and bushes are floating on clouds that wait and move obliviously, accepting their fate: evaporate and re-descend.

Lost in her own esoteria, Helen hears a noble sound in the forelands: a horse is going at a knightly stilled pace. It's Prince with Jim and Alli like one. They're naked again, or still, and the image is perfectly pure. After a ride, the warmth is lying on their skin.

Helen grows aware of the tree further down the fields, where sheep will be looking for shade, and she smiles.

Oh no, Mr. Satan, I won't eat the apples!

Just pick them?

No no, sly little devil, I won't touch them.

You don't want to know more?

Shut up; that knowledge is fatal.

About good and evil? Fusing into a godly whole?

With glowing muscles Jim and Alli are on their way home. Other parts of their bodies are heaving at Prince's gait, and Alli's hair is down in rocking waves.

Helen controls herself and waits in a daydream full of atmosphere.

Who, for God's sake, will avoid a collision?

All disconnecting pairs, narrowly missing tracks,
aren't scared in the least, since 'apart' means 'free'
and some rare safe happiness could presently vanish,

while two swans in the milder light
aren't floating aside but right in the waves,
where the biggest ships are steering clear for a bit.

Helen makes orange juice and takes it up to Jim and Alli's rooms. The latter is in the bath, singing softly, and he is languid on the sofa, reading a paper.

'Does a lilac sky promise good weather?' Helen asks solemnly.

With a towel coiled around her head, Alli comes in and Helen reacts once more: 'Can I take your pictures? The way it was this morning?'

'Don't be grotesque,' Jim says.

'For my new show!'

'Mum, it's ridiculous.'

'But don't you want to know what it's about?'

'No, woman, I want to live a moment in freedom, without *freezing* it.'

'Or a photo series on the track and field?'

'No, thanks, it's an ordeal to *dodge* the cameras.'

'And you?' she asks Alli, who's in a baggy robe.

And even if she wore a newspaper, she'd be eye-caressing: full-slim, a dark-light skin with a touch of velour, the music in her shoulders and arms.

Jim's radiance is also like that: with uncombed hair and slouched in his loose robe, he remains the top athlete, optimally developed. The way that comes from the inside, is what Helen would like to reveal if she had any idea, to feel or own yet what she's lacking.

'No,' says Alli, 'sorry.'

72

'Not even for Charity or a good cause? The most respected sport celebrities and Secretaries of State pose naked, to raise money for an orphanage in awful countries.'

Alli is thinking or visualizing, but Helen goes on. 'If you see what sort of sex there is on television, causing tragedy and confusion among children...?'

After a hesitance Alli says: 'Go and campaign against *that*!'

'Yeah,' Jim says, 'you've just collected from those networks.'

On the way back to her den, Helen attempts to have another comforting and realistic thought –

No shred of regret!
What it's about now, takes place in time,
because later or sooner here's the endless void containing all.

but the phone rings.

It's Romy. 'Oh, Mum, I'm scared.'

'What, babe, don't be ashamed, I'm a good listener, is it a man? Then I'll say one thing: go ahead, I mean, go live your own life, because there's... Rome? Honey, don't do any...'

She's hung up in the ancient payphone of New York's Terminal Station. She feels more miserable than many a prisoner, because 40th and 9th is avoided by Travel Shows, no matter how engrossing or unexpected or close the presenter wants to be between his breakfast and dinner in a star hotel far from here.

The hall proves to be so vast that for a long time Romy asks herself whether it's a place under or above ground in the dusk.

Finally she walks in the last outside daylight and holds her bag tight. Dodging the trash cans and piles of garbage beside them, she tries to ignore the burning cigarette butts or the eyes of people in doorways, while drivers are lurking along the curb.

A rusty brown fire escape seems to rub off.

She should have taken the Subway here. Who can see what she feels?

Eyes are stabbing her back.

She's not breathing and needs to pause, her arms and legs are numb, but she will reach Wyatt House on 34th, where the front desk has enough security bars. She doesn't look around, just pays for the week assigned by The Wise Girls PR management.

The triple-lock room is in a long corridor on the fourteenth floor. Romy unpacks her scant baggage and spreads a Manhattan map, when a bang like a bomb-hit strikes the walls. Baffled, she expects the screaming and running of casualties, but the silence is as deathly as before.

Cautiously she opens the window and looks down into the court, where layers of waste are buried under one another. On the other side a few people are leaning out, visibly under some influence.

When another blow hits the building, Romy can see that bottles are being thrown out of windows, and the crashes on the trash are echoed and magnified by four high walls, to haunt Romy's mind.

She lies down on the bed, where the sheets are clean and her headache fades into a sort of clairvoyant dream about the engine of life, not a season yacht.

On extensive waters
we're sailing together,
yet wholly independent
and waving in sympathy
to a girl on the empty shore,
who calls out and tries to speak,
but clearly she can't hear us at all;
what with the horse power we've got!
Poor little thing, she's left behind already.

Indeed, Romy is *meant* to feel bleak. Vexed by her 'ethical scruples', The Wise Girls find her a stuck-up and gutless traitor and send her on immediate leave after a mega event in the Olympic Arena of Montreal. Her stand-in will happily take over for an indefinite period of time. That should produce new commercial exposure for the group and give Rom the opportunity to distance herself and view priorities.

It's just like this juicy show stunt called 'Millionaire turns Homeless for one week'. A jet for the Caribbean goaded the paparazzi, while Romy was put on a rattling bus – outside the current publicity hype – to a specific part of a certain city without her phone, only one old-fashioned cheque, some cash and ragtag clothes, and the strict prohibition to contact any relative or Press person, as if you're not handicapped enough already without a smartphone. The thought of walking and talking to a tabloid is an attractive kind of suicide if career death is imminent. For the rest of your life they'd tap your phone and hack your computer. She even gets used to the bottle bangs, or she manages to ignore them for spells of sleep and a sense of exploring adventure, if not exactly the trendy sort from travel shows. Or immensely so? Who takes these life-making decisions about fashion and camp or crap?

All she can do now is lead a life of her own – and she can't remember how to do that, really.

Bewildered on a sober trip,
I long back for the palace
with the glow of a gold
that keeps no prisoner.

On the other side of the night it's a rude awakening to wash naked among hawking, sniffing, blowing women, all in moods of their own, but after that it's not so bad to choose the flights of stairs over a packed elevator.

Looking straight ahead and safely carrying her sparse valuables on her skin, she crosses the ground floor into the open, where the sun is relentless too.

Descending into an over-the-top sanctuary called The Village, Romy buys a grapefruit and finds a paper, then she sits on the antique basement steps of what could still be a stale artist's place.

In the paper there's no sensational story on The Girls.

Because no difference is noticed?

The grapefruit is bitter and that means it must be healthy. She takes her time to unwind by peeling each piece, neatly dropping the rinds and skins on the paper. A woman comes out who's more the executive than painter or writer type, but she doesn't even chase Romy away. Inspired by this decency, Romy drops the paper and waste in a bin.

Slowly she walks on, growing profoundly conscious of her freedom to wander and explore like this without photographers and bodyguards, without being recognised! She keeps pausing to let it sink in and believe.

The heat is blending with the sounds and smells of traffic, voices of the masses, perfumes and gasses and sirens of daily real life. Houston Street, Lafayette Street...

World-class literature like Joyce's *Ulysses* is loaded with local names, but Romy became famous before finishing school, so this is all very new to her.

Here's a place where the nation's trade is made, leading the world's economy or downfall. This narrow old street resembling The City in London? And suddenly, as if the wrong movie sets are built in the Studio of Life (no roles for pop stars now?), she can't remember her lines, just feels the burning of immense lights and lenses. A thousand extras come into action, almost trampling her.

Featuring in every News bulletin around the globe, it's closing time for the banks and Exchange: swarms of stern suits are moving to the Subways, and Romy escapes to the sacred building where a door is ajar and an organ sounds like August waves: Trinity Church.

Pressed on a wooden pew, drenched in the music, she closes her eyes and sees a dance pair whirling in delicate gauze clothing, slenderly floating along. They advance to the altar and return, each on a side of the pews. Down the aisles they go back and meet again, dancing on, parting and reuniting, driven and lifted faster and higher by the power of the organ chords, humbly triumphant, ending in the silence that she was looking for.

It's no delusion of despair, Romy knows, but a wistful wish dream, now that her feelings wake up after years of sedation, touched by music above time.

So I promise not to go looking for symbols I don't believe in.

The dusk of this edifice has soothed her eyes, and eagerly she breathes its coolness in, until the rush-hour noise obtrudes. She'd love to wait for the organist to play more, but people have warned her that the area is not safe when it's deserted after six.

**

The bike has stopped and the silence is a breath of nature. It's not even broken by the figure appearing in an arch of trembling leaves: he's *part* of nature. The sidelight is showing this child of Greek statues.

There's no tan or any outline of swim pants, but it's not an indoor whiteness, it's ivory or almond. There's little pubic hair, just lots of space with bulges and curves. His penis is thick and pushed up by the firmness of his balls. It's all so strongly drawn in the spring clearness of my yard – as if I'm putting my fingers on it.

Shading his eyes, he glances around. The lifting of his arm brings a series of muscle motion. The other hand is leaning on the hip. As he's skimming the house, I slip behind the curtains, although I'm sure he can't see me.

The gauze is tickling my skin.

He saunters around the lawn, passing by this open window, then he walks to my clothes, feels and smells them, and puts my shorts on. He smiles – first time – and takes a few funny hip-swaying steps. Next he sits in my chair, leans back and closes his eyes, as if it's always been like this, for better or worse. For the begging.

So I don't hurry. I make coffee and it will be the best handmade ever, with a couple of sandwiches. Let's put a lace cloth on the tray.

Concentrating, I walk down the wooden steps onto the grass, to put the tray beside the chair, spread my fresh towel on the other side of the tray, and take my clothes off, which are his, leaving the shorts, like him.

He's been watching.

I offer him the coffee and he also takes a sandwich.

I expected him to eat like a beast, but he's very neat.

'Thank you,' he says so suddenly and so normally that I can't react, paralyzed by the warmth of his voice. It's not very deep for a man but so rich and 'roundish' that those two words are a story of their own.

'My name's Brian,' he says.

'Warren. How are you?' As if we're meeting at a business reception. He puts his arms behind his head and stretches fully, lazily.

And now I don't think I'll be able to answer for myself any longer, I just have to touch these mini hairs in the sunshine on his arm. But when I'm reaching down, he stands up and stretches again, leaving some space for a finger between waist and shorts band, and he kneels on the big soft towel I've brought, to lie on his stomach at full length, his face turned away. So either he's unaware of what's going on in me or he's allowing and perhaps inviting me to take a close look.

I do, from the finest eyelashes to the tiniest mole on his Achilles' heel. How cute even the nails of his fingers are. An ant is climbing his neck and I follow its track with the tips of my lips – just like that.

He moves. But it's a slight motion. Is he trying to tell me that he doesn't mind anything?

The real ordeal:
biblical or political

Evidently a desolation
is different from a desert;
if only it's not forty years!
I'd turn into my own guide,
so at least he would hear me.

Don't lead us into temptation,
Lord, because you have no idea!

In the course of these days Romy buys a bunch of carrots and
chews them thoroughly, now strolling around, then sitting on a
bench or a piece of grass, in a bus crisscross along her pick of
district, and on a boat passing under the well-known bridges,
that she's always taking for the Golden Gates of places where she
gave concerts.

    Known to be great at sunset?

    Well, she never really got to see.

    Chewed until they're juicy, carrots are very nutritious, and
Romy buys cartons of milk, to drink them right away in the heat,
with dry bread. There's vitamin D or something in sunshine; even
here where nature is gone?

    She meets a tramp who shows her the Center of Charity &
Anarchism, but Liberty stays a statue. Together they steal clean
underwear and a piece of hot food, while gulls are screeching and
diving to pick large crumbs of all kinds from the ground, watched
hungrily by Romy and Bummy.

    The moments of stealing or finding things, offer some tension
and truth, the simplest highlights that Romy needs, because the
papers don't mention The Girls. Haven't they noticed her absence
at all?

    'I'm incognito,' she reveals to Bummy.

    'Ah, no make-up!'

'The Wise Girls call me a spoilt brat, and Management want this test for me, to learn about Life and Hard Times.'

'An initiation?'

'What's that?'

'Like the ancient Celts,' Bummy explains, 'dumped on the sea in a boat with no pedals.'

'No credit-cards!'

'Just surrender to the tide, taking you home or to a nasty slow death.'

Romy shrugs.

To keep fit, they walk as far as their energies allow it, arriving at a parking lot where they find a few coins by a meter. Crazy with joy they stamp their feet and flail their arms as if it's cold.

After an hour or so Bummy suggests a visit to the library.

'Why?'

'To do what celebs and politicians do: write a book.'

She learns that murderers get millions for their stories, which has become crime cause number one. The State has a share in the profits, helping to pay for prisons, which are too expensive with the endless extensions of Death Row, where the main parts of lives are spent, depending on a governor's moods against a lawyer's intelligence and stamina during the appeals and stays of execution.

After seven days of being human, Romy is lonely. Life with The Girls was no job but a former existence, and a new one is lacking. More than mental castigation or withdrawal symptoms, this is about stuff like death and re-birth, and she doesn't know how to cope with any of it.

Friday night her belongings are packed, the valuables on her chest, when it hits her that she forgot to cash the cheque, and some flashes of bare and banal facts are razor-sharp: banks closed in the weekend, no bed after tomorrow, cash spent to the last cent – that was the fun! – and no food or return ticket. If only, if only... She did pass by enough banks, had all the time. But it was exhilarating to be poor! She could have been so happy now if there was anywhere to go.

The fear is mixed with an anger that gives her the strength to think and act. At night some stores may be open, but banks? Not in this hood.

She inquires down at the desk. Uninterested, somebody says: 'Maybe tomorrow morning, downtown.'

She checks out the street, walks a few blocks, but it's getting dark.

Defying desperation, she'll try to sleep in case she'll need it. Surely some banks are open around the clock? Yeah, at airports! Why did they put her on a coach in Montreal? Well, a survival test would lead her to faith.

There's no mysticism left, though, only the dead-normal fact that she can't stay or go!

She can hear Bummy ask: So why don't you hitchhike?

Because I'm terrified! OK?

...to find herself in a bad spot, where cars can't really stop. After hours of angst here's an old truck, pulling over on the narrow grassy verge – out of pity? Soon it would have been too late, in the darkness.

Her voice is lost in the droning of the engine, as they thunder past stretches of desolation. The big and unwashed man is chewing and looking at her, encouraging, possessive.

When he gears down without visible reason and puts his broad hand on her leg, she knows it's nothing to do with her or him; it's the will of his flesh. But most animals are nobler.

He parks in the corner of a large lot.

No big deal.

He smiles with closed eyes.

Not only his unshaven chin hurts her.

She gets tired and dirty, and time is not alert or kind.

Saturday morning at eight there's no dime for breakfast.

She heads towards the main avenues, where it's painfully beautiful in this early freshness with bits of nature like a scrambling sparrow.

There's a long queue outside a bank, but when at last it's her turn, she learns that a Savings Bank doesn't take foreign cheques on Saturdays.

There are more queues like these, and she keeps trying against better judgement, until a sympathetic man wonders: 'No service in your hotel?'

No, maybe at the police station!

But he's given her a last-straw idea.

The hotels on Central Park South and Fifth Avenue are so formal and distinguished that Romy is afraid to go in, dreading a scene in front of a crowd or reporter. Pop stars, film stars and politicians have suites here as equals – for secretive excitement that may or may not be detected. So Security is grim, and she can't give her identity away, even if the sagging hair and bags under the eyes are a disguise by themselves.

Further up the Park is the friendlier front of Hotel Pierre. Ignoring her dirty nails and dusty clothes, she reaches Reception inconspicuously and waits by the sign CHANGE – freaking metaphorical or not.

When a young man looks at her, she asks: 'Will you please help me with a cheque? I've nowhere else to go.'

The embarrassment of this beggar-in-training is visibly real.

The man in livery tries not to eye her from head to foot, but his eyes act on their own. Whether he can't believe it (sweaty and torn top, worn jeans, a cheap wig to cover weirdness?) or he believes that it's the latest after-party rage for the famous and bored, or he's afraid of a situation like her.

At least he's intrigued; is this his life chance of a hero's role? The day has been eventless enough and here this creature comes in from the fringe or trendy art scene, needing a rescue.

She explains the ridiculous fix she's in, or a part of it, and this may be the classic, magic, romantic, heart-rending start of a brand new life (for both? Together?), an example of love's modesty and joy to many.

The good fellow is not quite ready for enlightenment or a life's upset just yet, he confers with his colleague and tells her the truth: 'We don't have the rates updates in the weekend.'

As realistically as possible she says: 'Take yesterday's rates, please, or ten percent lower!'

In the moment of breakthrough either way, he reflects and studies the cheque again, then runs it through the computer, presses keys and pays her, and will cherish her mad gratitude for a long time, with or without romantic regret.

Smack through traffic Romy dashes into the park, chatting to children on their ways to the Zoo, reminiscing the day she sang here for a hundred thousand. She jumps tree-high on the path to Greyhound Station and buys delicious food like rolls and cooled drinks.

At noon she gets on the coach, if not exactly home.

Over the engine's humming and fellow travellers' babbling, also during the stops for visits to clean and bright and quiet bathrooms, there's time to feel that the whole scare has been a good thing in the end, because it makes her all the happier now.

Last interview

When I do go on, I have to start anew,
an inward move, if the world is rescued.
With a smooth curve I could begin afresh.

It's like a bum's blog:
    Montreal, a mild night.
    Just wait for daily-life reality.
    Travellers are pushing backpacks around.
    St. Catherine Street, Boulevard de Maisonneuve…
    This funny medley of English and French; yes, she does remember.
    The Girls have returned from Toronto and Quebec; it's practical for Management to collect Romy here again, when or if they know where she is.
    Dorchester Boulevard.
    These names would be as real as pretty and good in a blog or book! Bored or forlorn, porn stars and Ministers and Murderers make fortunes with their stories as the basis of TV series that are sold to a hundred countries.
    'Capital punishment cannot give solace,' Romy types anonymously.
    'On death row our many years are precious,' tweet the many followers eagerly, 'hoping that the electric charge won't fail again, killing us only half.'
    After a death penalty the State share goes to the criminal's family, but investigations will not go too deep, since the State profits have never been higher – a necessity too, for the costly business.

Perhaps a bitter or blissful personal narrative could provide the right theme for Richard's PhD or 3D thesis: the post-modern coming-of-age egodocufiction?
    'Luckily the uni's keep their billions of subsidies.'

'Yeah, what would Health Care do with those?'For detailed research Rich visits a syntho-addiction group in the Betty Ford House 46, where guests can make efforts to be sincere, on the sole way to curing obsessions like porn, gym fitness, travelling, The News, and beauty surgery with huge painkillers. Elbowing to take the floor, they push borders of self-help through mindfulness.

'Back in a minute for the sex issue; stay with us!'

'*The Weather Forecast* could be cut down, after the ocean temperature in parts of the world that would be good for sun-fun holidays.'

'And as to hefty sex...'

Yes, our attention is back.

Rich is fairly troubled by the openness of some people, like this person who got married, conceived four children, conquered Mont Blanc... and now changes genders.

'I'd never do that,' says the gym junkie. 'As if a man finds you attractive then!'

'Can be treated,' says a baby addict. 'It's often a cop-out from a failing marriage. Pay some attention to your kids! You'll feel a whole lot better.'

Helen can see Rich's inner conflict – he's torn – and she says: 'If you teach Dono how to ride a bike, the father experience will be sheer healing.'

He's fearful, but OK.

At age five Dono rides a digitronic tractor his size, so the stage of aid wheels can be skipped. 'No speeds for now, though,' the Raleigh man advises, and when Dono sways and swirls during a test ride, he thinks: the boy is disabled. Or crudely honest: he waddles like a spastic.

Helen can't help seeing that herself. 'But note his perception and observation: so mature!'

'Yes, pretty scrutinizing.'

She thinks not out loud: are his *motor* skills defective?

To balance out so much intellect?

Then what will swim classes be like?

And Rich knows just as quietly: endless hours (always at dinner time) in that chlorine pool full of snotty and snivelling and shivering children of chattering, wine-sipping parents behind the glass wall of the smoky canteen.

Watch other people's kid dripping in a queue on the diving board?

No thanks. Rich doesn't need second or third chances for his inner or any other child.

Practising the backstroke, Dono is bobbing and colliding in circles or diagonals around the whole pool, plumb through lines of kids and ropes. What a merciful circumstance that a pensioned volunteer looks out for him in the water.

Endearingly uneasy, Rich does help with the bike lessons, though: balancing, staggering, steering. He perseveres and even enjoys himself, becomes young and energetic again, almost feels a bond with the boy, who's lovingly grateful.

Joyous, Helen praises Rich's sensitive manliness, making him feel more torn than ever, so that he visits the Confusion Support Group in spite of himself, called *Confession Blog* in self-mockery, where the assignments are a bigger confrontation as they come closer to a truth.

III

dense openness
in tense hope

'... the quality of the pips,
which we had to plant with such care,
depended so to speak on how we ate the flesh.'
Marianne Fredriksson

Infinite optimist

On and often I'm dying
to make a fearless beginning;
no big strings attached, naturally.

Clearly I've been too dumb.
Surely it was caused by something
I'm certainly able to deal with completely.

Soon after sending him to school, Helen has a visit from headmaster Benedict, a special-spectacled and respectable man who shakes hands, wipes his glasses and states that something is wrong: 'Doneus fails at anything regular like English or Maths, but at the same time, without being told or asked, he makes a sort of speech about Third-World Aid or British Royalty as if they're connected, as if he's a direct descendent!'

And taking Benedict's coat in style, 'Tea?' Helen's smile is polite indeed, slightly distant or regal.

Benedict settles on the sofa. 'Our doctor and remedial teacher conclude in all simplicity that the causal-provisional prognosis is nil. The boy is a fluttering and flopping butterfly. By the *look* of it he seems almost normal, but the *in*visible... That remains to be seen.'

Helen makes noise in the kitchen and humbly offers the headmaster a plate of exquisite chocolates, but he continues considerately. 'Doneus has done some tests or tasks, and the scores are minimal.'

Helen retorts: 'Alright, highly gifted people have been known to fail the best IQ tests at standard schools. Like Escher!'

'Who's that?'

'Why, Escher made paintings and became famous!'

'And your son has this depth of sight or vision? It's more like a *blind* spot.'

'It's artistic or spiritual. How does your remedial teacher work?'

'Oh, let's hope the blindness will be something temporary. We'll keep an eye on him.'

And moved by that, Helen ventures to ask: 'How is he in class?'

'Ah, the little Beaumond – that is his name, I assume? He's more out than in.'

'Why?'

'He's either slow or fast!'

And Helen asks: 'But no misconduct?'

'Oh, he never joins in the general spitting and kicking.'

'No pushing and bullying or the usual psychological terrorism?'

'Well, he's more like an outcast,' Benedict says.

'Or a gifted drifter,' Helen tries.

'You mean: alienated from himself! You should be afraid to leave him at school; he's so alone, it's eating me.'

'Sure,' Helen says, 'I've read this famous, innovative book about kids who are *dys*lexic because they have a *mys*tical mission.'

'Which is?'

'They expose the weak spots of society.'

As Benedict raises his brows, Helen explains: 'The mania of Scoring and Performing! In an esoteric way these children rise in protest.'

'Utterly unconscious, of course?' Benedict interrupts.

'Well, kids go to school at an early age or to Day Care with educational baby TV and playful Internet.'

'But is he even incarnated?'

'Ah, I can understand a country's fear to fall behind other nations, who'd gain power then, but Dono should be no victim of this *ir*rational and restricted, *dis*proportional shit system.'

On the doorstep headmaster Benedict cleans and adjusts his remarkable glasses and says: 'Take the kid to a therapist, an incarnation specialist.'

All the lights are on, as far as they can go.
The house is not empty when I'm awake.
Guilt may be hiding or lying in ambush.

After a month or so the remedial teacher loses heart and refers them to an outstanding orthopeda coach: Xantha Wahlinger Van Aldenwood, who's featured in a magazine with her picture and all, and her husband Culius is a psychologist, so the results they book are always good.

'Is she gentility or is that her maiden name used for the sake of completeness?'

The RT really doesn't know.

'Never mind,' Helen says, and she makes an appointment right away.

It's a stiff car trip to a large and magnificent, perfectly converted farm building lying off the road so far that Helen misses the gate three times and fights the odd or obtrusive symbolism of it all. The sizeable fee per hour is not covered by any insurance, but Xantha's track record and skills radiate through her taste of clothes and hospitality. In order to put Dono at ease, she shows him and Helen the whole house first, then the grand consulting room and waiting room for parents.

The latter, with a relaxing artist's easel, is factually an office for Culius, whose foreign master's degree is not even recognized here!

The waiting-room view is so pastoral or rural ('rustic,' says Xan by mistake, blushing and mumbling some gutsy pun about dyslexia being inevitable with names like hers) that Helen gets restless, waiting during the long and expensive sessions.

With inward-looking eyes, Dono shows what he's built in therapy: a house with animals and people on a journey.

'Do they live in that house on the way?' Helen would like to ask. 'Or is that where they come home?' But for some thoughtful reason, she won't disturb him in that little world of his.

Xan is thrilled with his susceptibility to her special method of Expressing the Inside, and already she can state, while Dono is walking over to chickens on the other side of the yard, that nothing is wrong with his brain.

Happy, they drive off and Helen asks: 'Did you like it?'

'Yes, can I go again?'

Oh, look at his eyes! If they really mirror the soul, could he be *too* susceptible: to things *out*side daily life?

To incarnate better, he'll go seventeen times, growing a lot quieter, but one late Autumn day during an evaluating parent session, Xan has a worrying message: 'In the houses Dono builds, the father is always absent and the mother is often tired.'

'Yes,' Helen says tearfully, 'because I need to be a mum and dad at the same time!'

'What's more, the houses are never in the same spot.'

Oh, there we go, Helen admits in silence: it's what drove Jimmy nuts already.

Is the little guy trying to build an Ark because the people around him are so bad, or as a measure to rescue the climate?

No, this is a great deal worse: 'Dono doesn't feel at home anywhere, that is, he's not grounded, let alone rooted. Sadly the treatment of such disorders is extremely hard.'

'How come?' Helen wants to know, sick to the stomach.

'I'm not sure; it's a complex case.'

'But it's your job!'

'No, this goes much further. I'm referring you to psychiatrist Stellinger. He collaborates with me well and the costs are covered or deductible. He may be very direct, close to bluntness, but he's terribly clever, so you'll learn to deal with that.'

Helen feels like smacking the easel, on which an unfinished painting has sat for seventeen weeks, but she receives Stellinger's details and says goodbye to Xan, whose own son is at a school for special education and even he finds it strange that Dono asked for a chicken – to take home.

In the car on her way back along the landscape that Helen loves one day less than the other, she philosophises: did Rich

94

teach him how to ride a bike too early, and is that why he's got this father complex?

In the baby years all important matters got her careful attention: no television set very close to the crib (like in most homes), no glaring lights or constant photo flashes, plenty of clean diapers, fresh air and sleep (she left him in peace out there for hours!), toys without beads and no flabby dolls until he could stand on his own feet, only useful games, unless... She did have doubts about the quick perpetuum mobile and hip music over his head, that seemed to make him sleep nice and easily, as if exhausted. But all kids have one! So he's abnormal?

It's all so harrowing if repairs can't be made anymore!

Bursting into a sweat, she needs to stop and get out. Is Xan giving her a remorse trauma because she's got a syndrome or complex herself? Why else would she claim that Dono is an *extra*ordinary child? That must be projection or a compensation for some fat crap!

On the elevated road she's catching the wind.

Cold.

Or bright, clear and crisp?

The last cows are being collected from the meadows. One of them is resisting heftily and gets beaten with a stick. Maybe the heavy animal can feel where it's going.

Yes, Helen is pleased that she's no cow or farmer.

What a dark frosty sky there over the water! If the roads freeze over, the dike would be a dangerous place for driving. What helps to compose herself is the necessity to stay alert and responsible for Dono's sake. It will be hard work to put his life in the proper direction.

Just on time she does get home before he's back from school.

To be on the safe side she gives him a snack without artificial aromas, liquorice without the colourings that make him hyperactive, a wholegrain biscuit and pure juice instead of the cola that affects his teeth enamel.

All details have been on school television.

Within ten years they may discover that such artificial additives also affect the nerves and brain. The crazier the process, the later its cause is traced. So many children have behavioural problems!

'Hi, darling, how was it today?'

She removes a sweet stray of hair from his fatigued brow.

'Good, we've done drawings.'

'Oh, what sort?'

'We did portraits, painting each other.'

'Lovely! I mean, how did it go?'

'Good. I was with George, and nobody really tried.'

'The others? What did they do?'

'The others made fun.'

'And you?'

'I was earnest.'

'See now?' Helen explains to Richard. '*Serious* words and assignments are fine! Mark *my* words.'

Still Rich won't take Dono to swim classes. He will not blame himself either, afraid of guilt on his shoulders, because most neck and back pains can be related to that sort of inner burden.

'Doctors keep talking about the early wear and tear of this or that, whereas it's often about the parasympathicus of the autonomous nervous system, which should prevent so many problems.'

This report made by objective and media-shy physicians would change the whole business of Insurance: a lot of employees would become redundant there. So better not read it.

To pause and reflect for a sec

Is this all, these days: we save the peace?
Surely you've got enough of that now?
Let's collect something totally new!

These days Jim is known as Jimpics, who'll win the gold at the next Games, and he doesn't really need what Rich reads, however true. The parasympathicus is improved by natural relaxing, and that's exactly what Jim does frequently, how odd it may sound, although he dislikes the indoor season, which is long here.

To him the 60m is a piddling distance: his ligaments are killed by the perennial bends of indoor runs, and he misses the fresh air, where sounds do not rebound into permanent noise.

'*What* sounds?' a reporter asks.

'The endless shouting of presenters, attempting to add Fun & Facts.'

'To what, for God's sake?'

'To the sheer joy of the sport itself.'

Bewildered by this raw emotionality, the press man reclines.

In any case, Jim receives more and more invitations for events in warmer continents.

Alli's concert career is equally international, and sometimes she misses him so much that it hurts even physically, after a competition or concert, when satisfaction asks for tenderness and sharing.

For Alli it's almost easy to withdraw into a dressing room, a practice room or outdoors in one of the old parks that are often near splendid concert halls. Her press interviews are quiet and reasonably brief. Taxis take her to spots where tourists and networks don't go. But professional athletics are very different. Even if the Decathlon is mostly still about sport, with a true comradeship, for Jim it's difficult to find the necessary peace.

When he's reading a book in the field, other athletes are surprised, making jokes, and one or two may laugh at him, but he can get used to that and in the course of two days they're too tired to be funny, while reporters find it increasingly peculiar, if intriguing. The fact that somebody leafs through a magazine is just about OK, but a book like a *novel* or, God forbid, *poetry*...

They sneak up on this reading Beaumond, who's getting more space on the sports page of some papers than the Royal Hundred Meters, which in fact is poetic justice to the Decathlon. His personality is called 'charismatic yet enigmatic'.

On the long two days, Jim blows air out and rubs muscles, cheers and makes fists, changes clothes and shoes, tends wounds and equipment quite normally, still the pauses between performances can be wearying when he hears too much again; then a spell of reading is a perfect way of de-tension. He knows that the mind is mainly the area where the essence of sports takes place.

They give him new nicknames like 'guru', and during the compulsory interviews he's asked the most intelligent and original questions:

'Are you happy?'

'Yes.'

'Will you win tomorrow too?'

'Don't know yet.'

'Did you expect this?'

'No, although I have trained a lot.'

'Should each training camp have yoga or meditation?'

'Yes, if training camps must be...'

'Why yoga?'

'It's good for body and soul.'

'Which helps?'

'Yes.'

'With results?' checks the desperate reporter.

'Definitely.'

'How come?'

'Well, it brings peace and strength, and tact or patience with stamina.'

'To everybody?'

'Yes, ma'am.'

'But what if *everybody* runs PB's?'

'Then it makes no difference.'

'But Jimmy, competition will stay just as big.'

'Or it will shrink, for more pleasure and better health.'

For a second all expectant reporters are struck dumb; they watch him accusingly because their time is up and they can't ask about world records anymore.

In a tasteful and comfortable hotel lounge, a renowned French journalist called Aramant has arranged to meet Allison, who is in a deep chair, wearing jeans and trainers. Throughout the conversation she remains calm and charming, modestly benevolent.

'It seems to me,' Aramant begins, 'that you're too young to travel so much, even for these world-class concerts.'

'Yes.'

After waiting for elaboration in vain: 'So?'

'I don't, really.'

'Pardon?'

'On the average I travel only once a week.'

'And the rest of the time?'

'Well, I often stay at home.'

'To do what?'

'Study or read and be happy with friends and family.'

'I see. Is your Beaumond friend always there?'

'No.'

'Ah, is that painful?'

'Yes.'

'Then how are you coping?'

Allison is wistful. 'With patience, work, love. And sometimes the longing can be even more sublime than consuming.'

She means coitus? wonders the right-minded man.

'So what if it becomes physically... unbearable?'

'Oh, I cry and write and... surrender.'

'To what?'

'The sadness.'

To which he can't add another word.

Alli would like to call Romy and hear how she deals with deep interviews, but neither the managers and agents nor publicists or The Girls themselves know where Romy is.

Due to the email mounts, a paper note is not found until days later. It says that she's going into a retreat in order to write a moving and suspenseful novel – with pen and paper, seemingly, because it's been ages now – but there are no contact details.

Slowly,
on its own,
blooming far
at a pure height
above all disbelief,
this flower is growing...
until it's touched by the light.

Rebellious, Helen doubts the use of seeing Stellinger. Dono has learned how to swim! It's a little higgledy-piggledy, but that indicates his groundbreaking nature! She will not, for that matter, become a pathetic and pathologic therapist hopper in a posh and busy part of town where it's hard to find a parking place. However, she does feel her responsibility again and makes an intake appointment.

Efficiently Stellinger follows a clear and forceful questionnaire about Dono and his next of kin, and Helen's replies – all non-verbal or explicit signals – are noted with sufficient space for interpretations.

'Any admissions in hospitals or clinics?'

'Um... No...'

'Has the boy known unconscious tension?'

'Not that I know of.'

'His phases of sitting, crawling and walking have been normal?'

'And falling, absolutely, as normal as can be.'

'As can be expected in the circumstances. OK. Any foreigners in the family?'

'Is that a good thing?' Helen checks eagerly.

'Well, if a child is confused by two languages, they can cause more dyslexia or disharmony.'

'Ooh.'

'Homosexual parents?'

'The *natural* ones? I mean...'

Does a stepdad count if he knows?

'Good, let's have him in.'

However rude Stellinger's quickness and candour may be, 'Your son has a serious brain or other blockade, perhaps rooted pre-natally,' the minute he speaks with Dono, his expertise is confirmed.

Helen opens the door and lets Dono in. Unsuspectingly he takes Helen's seat and loyally she stands behind him at some distance.

'How old are you?' Stellinger asks.

'Five years. How many months in a year?'

'Well, twelve!' Stellinger says impulsively.

'For how long?' Dono inquires.

'Oh, very long.'

And Helen is nodding approvingly but looks worried when her youngest goes on: 'From the Middle Age?'

'Certainly,' Stellinger answers.

'But won't that change?'

'Why?'

With intense hope Helen looks from one to the other.

'On Sunday,' Dono says, 'the time changed an hour – back – and the phone is very different.'

'See?' Stellinger tells Helen in all honesty after gaping at Dono. 'This kid is in trouble.'

In a weird silence the specialist brings up aspects of Dono that will be fatal in puberty. 'It's too big a risk to start a psycho therapy that might fail after a year.'

And Helen feels an icy coldness clutching her soul when he advises extensive clinic admission: 'Do you understand? We have eminent contacts in youth homes.'

She's unable to answer, so with the utmost sympathy he continues: 'That will *add* a trauma first, I'm aware of that, but it's calculated, and in fact you have no choice – to avoid more disaster later.'

The man is distressed himself, although he's experienced enough.

By now Helen understands that something drastic is expected of her, but even deeper inside she knows that a clinic is off limits; it's more or less where he came from!

Imagine taking him to a remote place with no knapsack full of cuddly toys – memories not allowed. She'll have to find a radical alternative. Going against an expert's advice? In an area where parents only make mistakes? What a superior task!

Safe back home, Helen longs for something courageous and active, clean and sweet, just what Dono's hair-wash offers: a soft cloth on his eyes, a pile of dry ones at hand, the water nice and warm, spraying it on his back first. This chore used to be a struggle and annoyance, now it's turned into a ritual of TLC.

'What's a son of a bitch?' Dono asks casually or kinesiologically.

Helen has trouble doing two things at the same time, and some suds get into his eyes. 'Hold on.'

After drying off, he repeats the question instead of forgetting it, as she hoped.

'Who told you?' she stammers.

'Kids at school.'

'What else do they say?'

'They'll kick my balls. What are my balls?'

'Well, you know, better ask Jim or Rich; it's really a men's question.'

He'd prefer Jim, but the brother is at a Grand Prix in Spain.

'It's the flesh and blood balls,' Rich tries paternally, 'that go with your willy. When you grow up even more, there will be seeds in them, for babies.'

'Oh. Are you saving them?' Dono asks.

Under an innocent silly kid's misapprehension that the stock or reserve was not recurrent, Richard stopped masturbating for a long while in his teen years. To prevent any anguish of conscience, still very familiar, he feels obliged to do some explaining, especially about no running out of semen.

'Sweet,' Dono says after listening.

And it's made them buddies already, Helen perceives in the course of weeks.

who wants to be first.

Has the light intensified
even more than it shines?
In the end – apparently –
on the glides of wings
that no one can carry
till the borders fade
for the very last

Rich nearly finishes his PhD at Layham University, about the Culturalistic Ambiguity in Contemporary Narratology. But a part of the dissertation is rejected. Although his original vision of the psycho-composition in Warren Leavitt's work is regarded as excellent, the *subsidiary* literature is deemed insufficient.

'Because it doesn't exist yet!' Rich explains and complains in the support group. 'I'm *creating* it. That's the job of a scholar!'

'What then is your primary structuralistic principle?'

'Erotic energy mainly occurs between poles.'

'Hm, like electricity.'

Here's a charged and edgy hush. And exceptionally one of the coaches intervenes with a question: 'Is the sexual charge between gays less great than among straights?'

'That's the essential case.'

'Where all happiness or frustration begins.'

'You mean flirtation?'

'With or without aids.'

'Not anymore! You are old!'

'You know, most gays are honestly or secretly attracted to straights. It's nature's yummy force of opposites.'

'Bastard!' a young guy shouts at Rich.

Someone shakes his hips derisively.

Another shakes the head hesitantly.

'Ah, you're denying it? Your crotch on fire and your mind in the mud?'

'Thing is, most homo's would kill to be loved by a hetero, but it's agony to admit it.'

'It's a plain *flaw* of nature!'

'Even physically it doesn't fit very well, does it! That's proof! We should face the sadness and be brave.'

The coach's camera runs fast, while shocking phrases are blurted out everywhere. He can't even follow who is crying out what anymore, letting them be on purpose, for a merciful mental and anonymous cleansing:

'It hurts – unfair – the tailpiece of love – all in the genes – except if you can submit – not *bad*, but I'm so sad about it.'

'*Even if* you call it a mistake or deviation...

'Aberration...

'Defect?'

'Exception or discrepancy.'

'It's all incontestably present *within* human nature.'

'Some given visual fact as a part of creation?'

'It *belongs*.'

'Just as much as diabetes, leukaemia or anaemia?'

'Please, make it amnesia for me.'

'At least we don't invent any of it, do we.'

'Let's first accept it and then see what's to be done.'

'Pray and ask the pope.'

'As if one's nature is a deliberate choice!'

'Ask the pope what?'

'Why sex abuse by priests has been common for ages.'

'Maybe anything physical mirrors an aspect of the soul.'

'Because it grows around it? As a *law* of nature?'

'Yes, it's all a *result* of love.'

'So when two men or two women love each other dearly and physical, they can't help it.'

'Love comes from God, obviously.'

'With or without aids instead of a baby?'

'Come on, God makes no mistakes.'

'Neither does the devil. Together they create huge karmic options!'

'And gays can help nature a bit against overpopulation.'

'Go to hell.'

'But there must have been a pair in Noah's Ark too, invited!'

'Precisely my point: homosexuality does belong, as *something else*.'

The Pairs,
Life in hand?

There are whispers,
'figure skating is for sissies,'
but they do risky lifts at high speed,
and the final figure will be a 'death spiral',
taking the strength and timing and trust of a giant,
while thousands are watching nearby, millions worldwide.
As he is spinning, her head is hanging half an inch above the ice.
His limbs and mind are tired, straining past the limit, but he is no quitter.

With a lump in their throats, Jim and Alli are watching a pair who don't win a medal in Figure skating.

They ride to a song by Sinead O'Connor, and the harmony is so natural that it seems to be made for them. The combination of strength and sensitivity is such that you don't even hear the blades on the ice. The jumps and spins are fully synchronized while you can't see them paying attention. The whole programme is one motion of rhythm and lines: a lemniscate of gliding with a dance in the heart. The way they reach and float, lift and land, is a fusion of dance and sport, so the judges are muddled, blind to the fine control, the technique and courage with which they let go in a moment of total dependence.

The gift: sender admits

At last here's the nickname,
so funny that you laugh tears.

The parcels were pretty enough,
but one wrapping was transparent.

In the Beaumond era of athletics, every event has a Decathlon. Even when the crème de la crème is taking part, Jim can win a tournament so smoothly and beautifully that journalists ask him: 'What's your secret?'

'You mean, my hair?'

'Ah, the new Samson! And will Delilah betray you?'

A lady walks up and makes cutting motions by his head. 'Who could seduce you?'

'Me?'

The press room is crowded. Trainers and managers of other young athletes grumble about the one-sided attention. Working towards The Games, MondiSport won't even broadcast a Grand Prix anymore if Jim is not in it. He could ask big entry fees, but the element of competition is already in a vicious circle, since unlike most he needn't work for a living, beside the Decathlon. He's raised the sport to fabulous heights, and for each photo or juicy story or television appearance, apart from the smart compulsory interviews, a fortune is on offer.

'Which woman could seduce and ruin you like a daring biblical parable?'

Frowning, Jim looks around. Some laugh, others hold their breaths.

'Which man?' somebody asks, languishing or recalcitrant.

Apologetically Jim shakes his head.

'Do you take a lot of pills?' a man cries without raising his hand.

'Ask the doping officials.'

'Vitamins?'

Jim remains fearfully calm. 'A to G, in balanced food.'

'What about abstinence?'

'Not a drop.'

'And sexually?'

'Seriously. There lies my power.'

'Is it true that sex can drain energies?'

'Or it can make them flow.'

In a deathly silence phones and laptops are working like mad. Then: 'Any wedding plans?'

'Well... Would it make a difference? I love her so much already.'

Impolitely he checks his watch and stops talking, so tongues and fingertips can add whatever they think, for the next best-selling editorial.

Network executives attempt to carry off the Beaumond rights. Ever since the Helen case (she keeps firing the cam crews), fines for a breach of contract have risen considerably, and current Rights prices hit the sky after stories about Dono, made public in ripe and billable doses by one of his teachers.

No word from Romy, despite the large-scale searches by managers and editors, even more acutely than by the police and relatives this time.

Evil tongues claim that it's 'an abduction for real now'.

'Serves her right that nobody believes her anymore.'

After heaps of leafing and browsing, Helen finds the only solid alternative for Dono's clinic treatment: a re-incarnation therapy. That does frighten her, even though the therapist is called Joy of all names, who has a Masters in psychology and was a PE teacher in special education. With a firm and earthly voice she's no cloudy type at all.

After two visits Dono's sleeping problems are over, and in daytime he reacts to normal instructions like *Wipe your feet* or *Shoes off* and *Coat on a peg, please.* He's keen on the weekly sessions – or consultations, as Helen prefers to call them – and he doesn't like the holiday breaks.

Helen has picked a path of life that offers no physical guarantees. Will she ever with messy and desperate regrets knock on Stellinger's door again to be rejected harshly? For example if re-incarnation turns out to be a smoke screen and Dono becomes a dopey teen?

What's this biblical parable again, about the foolish girls who have no oil for their lamps...? She's always found that so unjust: a story with a warning coming too late.

One evening he's being pricked by a 'sting-beast'.

'A gnat?' Helen asks. 'Can't be.'

He shows her the bite bulge.

'Oh, then it must have wintered here.'

'A Dad Gnat?' the lad asks.

She wavers and evades this. 'Shall I put some ointment on?'

'But that will come off in the bath.'

'Well, you can let it absorb a bit and then it's done the job.'

That brings an enchanting grin to his face.

'What's up?' she asks.

'The way you say that!'

There are more moments like these, when she thinks to herself: what's going on in this mind or soul of his? For how long will it lie low?

The 'father gnat' keeps bugging her, but with a whole basket of food and goodies they tackle the long and busy drive to Joy each week, rising to some occasion where Life gains momentum in a sequence of rapids.

Joy sticks loyally to professional confidentiality, and after visits Dono is never talkative, so Helen respects that reverently, afraid to stir up anything too harrowing. Previous lives or karma and such are holy to her; she wouldn't dare interfere out of mere curiosity. Enlightenment may consist of blind acceptance!

Dono is growing deferentially quiet and wise.

Ultimately in spring, all three feel that it's 'done' here with Joy. On the last way back, both Dono and Helen are as happy as any newborn in the meadows, although saying goodbye to Joy was quite wistful.

A great deal has changed, except school results. While the government enunciates that children are amenable to something at the earliest age, which should be made the most of before it's too late, Dono still doesn't know what six plus five is.

Joy confirmed that Dono's brain is good; under hypnosis he can do maths with his eyes closed! So why not in class or at home and in shops? If the pedasophical book is correct (the one Helen read) and Dono exposes a shortcoming of society in the most profound and subtle way...

'Yes,' Helen tells the teacher, 'he excels in that as well! Am I supposed to be up to such a mission? What a position of honour and trust.'

To the most erudite and practical experts just like Joy, it goes without saying – the way a plant grows towards the light – that in the spiritual dimension souls choose their future parents, if willy-nilly sometimes.

'According to universal nature, we always end up there where the right soul work awaits us, to make us stronger and more conscious, and often it only *seems* to be the opposite, obviously, because resistance paves a journey of learning.'

Recently Helen has noticed by accident how much she loves Dono. One tabloid calls it sentimental, but she can't help thinking that her entire family has this mental depth.

Rich gives up his studies to pursue his heart without knowing what that may entail and whether it will work. With that surrender to the Supreme or perhaps to the Mud and Mire that shouldn't be skipped, it's just as if his heart never opened until now.

He collects Dono from school and can feel that the day here has been too long for the boy, as for most kids actually. Pale, yawning and lean, they come out carrying handicraft that also nearly breaks. They have trouble finding their bikes or minders who babble and cram the exit.

'On the bike, will you push me?' Dono asks when the jumble of adults is disentangled.

But it's such a renowned school that numerous children are brought and fetched by car from far, also driving there where the cycling track alongside is narrow.

'Watch the handlebars,' Dono says, when Rich leans over to put a hand on his shoulder and push him along gently, talking simultaneously.

'How was it today?'

'Good. I was in another room again.'

'With other children?'

'No, alone.'

'Did that help?'

'Don't know. I've got to see the school doctor again.'

'Oh. And has the special teacher been in?'

Dono hesitates. 'In and out.'

Rich stops asking whether it helps. As soon as there's a moment without a car passing by close, he takes a breath; at present he has such a need for fresh air!

'I've learned about the farm,' Dono says, 'on school TV. Can we go to the farm some day? But all the animals are stuck in a tight place; a thousand hundred locked up for life.'

'Not a *long* life, mind.'

'Watch your handlebars.'

How to push a little boy and keep a safe distance at the same time when you have a cool sports bike and he a clumsy low thing? It gives him a pain in the back with a lame arm. Still Rich says: 'We'll go and see animals that have all the space they need.'

'Tomorrow?'

'Well, no, it needs a bit of time.'

'When?'

'On a perfect cycling day in the holidays, OK?'

'I hope so,' Dono says. 'Because at school they call me "Don't know". Watch the handlebars. Am I from another country? Like very foreign?'

'Well, you seem to be here now. We'll call you *Do*, rhyming to *Joe*, alright? It's a music name.'

Unobtrusively he looks aside to see if Do may know more about his origins. Rich has no idea how straight Helen has been about certain family matters. If she lets 'nature' take its course in this respect, the tension could extend endlessly.

'Nah,' Do goes on musing, 'I don't *speak* funny and foreign, so…. Watch out.'

Their handlebars have touched and stay stuck in a stupid way. Rich's hand is still on Do's back. They're not pedalling anymore, and they're also afraid to brake. On one side cars are racing by, and on the other runs barbed wire. Frozen, they roll on and look in front of them; unable to say or do anything when so little and so much can happen.

This goes wrong, Rich knows crystal-sharply, now that he's watching himself during the sort of near-death experience. Balancing on millimetres, they hold and float in a pending poise. He can feel it giving way even before the crash in blackness, but in a curious form of resignation it's no fatal spill, the way you seldom break a bone when you faint.

The true shock doesn't come till after, as if he's really been out of his body and got hurled back into it full of pain and shame.

They're several yards apart without knowing how that came about. Do is the first to sit up on the pavement, beside his bike in a funny angle. Full of concern he looks at Rich rubbing his limbs and wincing.

'Are you painful?' Do asks.

'Not too bad, I think. You?'

'No. My jeans are bleeding.'

He's examining the knee and bloody hole, but Rich needs to wait for the lightness of head to subside. When his nerves are listening to the brain again, he scrambles up with involuntary moaning and mumbling: 'Come on, old man.'

He limps over to the stepson, who picks up his bike and asks: 'Are you broken?'

'Certainly not, just a bit bruised and stiff.'

Crooked and stooped but in one piece, Rich is now laughing more than he has in years. 'Have mercy!'

Relief and gratitude make him realize that God has a devilish sense of humour.

Who glows

Was I just going,
to show you myself...
here you are at the door!

In the broad outer windowsill
a small sun has warmed the snow.

The wounds are tended and the story is told for the most part:
　　'Just *beside* the barbed wire...'
　　'A car screeched and braked on time.'
　　'We escaped from a camera...'
　　Do's knee will have a little scar that girls may find sexy tough.
Rich will be slightly crippled for the rest of his life, despite a series
of treatments by the osteopath, and in the Confusion Support
Group someone asks: 'Is this punishment?'
　　Rich is fed up with the sessions. 'It's like sharing hour in Do's
class, damn it.'
　　But the subject is changed diplomatically: 'How come the
ancient Greeks did sports in the nude?'
　　For a moment it makes Rich wayward and sullen. 'Were they
jumping the hurdles then?'
　　'OK, come on!' they cheer. 'Give it all, Rich, and let some hair
down: manifest yourself!'

He goes to watch the training sprees in Jim's arena, and he visits
the largest Gay Manifestation in the country, with a parade,
info market, swing party with a boys band and a girls band,
ecumenical celebration and choir festival. He's even booked a
camping place, but he cancels that. Unbiased in the happy crowd,
anyone's obscure or suppressed sides appeal to him less and less.
　　There's also a sort of regret: 'Our Do is not my child.'
　　Yet forgiving by nature, Helen says: 'It's never too late for
good.'
　　Pale, he stammers, 'No...'

'For example, you can take Do to that school doctor or *I* will be the patient. Those people make me phobic: *one* expert wants him in a Home; the next calls him a psychic in retro-carnation. Please, let it be his *final* incarnation. Unless he'll be the next dalai lama, of course. About time too.'

Helen is sprawled on the sofa with a deep-freeze pack on her forehead. Richard is pacing classically and Dono is at the table to make a sandwich, listening to the grown-ups and watching with wide clear eyes even as he's handling the knife to spread peanut butter.

'Please, Rich,' Helen insists. 'Take pity and take care of him.'

'But I'd never finish my book!'

'About The Loss of Soul in Literature? While Do may be locked up for life? How dare you compare and complain! After the shock of a crash it's always best to return and conquer fears immediately.'

So comradely 'the men' get on their bikes again.

Doctor Bogard is wearing no stethoscope but low spectacles, while his assistant, Saskia, has a chart and files. On the walls are posters with eyesight tests and Chinese or Tibetan characters.

'Hello there,' Doc begins jovially, 'how are you?' (Do tries to answer.) 'My assistant will do little games with you, and I can have a chat with your dad.'

As Do is astonished, Saskia hands a chart to the physician.

'Ah...'

'I'm his mother's husband,' Rich helps, shaking hands.

'Hm, I believe this lad is in a rough patch.'

Saskia takes Do four yards away, within the hearing distance of normal people, although Doctor Bogard does lower his voice a bit ominously. Do obliges the assistant by bending, walking on a line, squinting and pointing.

'His progression is nil,' Bogard states. 'He needs attention, and a school for special education has facilities, less large groups, adapted methods, anyway, you must know that.'

Knowing what it takes to obtain a place there, where insecurity is compensated by all sorts, taken out on timid peers, to be misunderstood by the heart-warming teachers, Rich is genuinely upset. 'Do is a sensitive boy; can it be that he needs more time?'

'Mr. Beaumond, we'd love to grant him that, and we're horribly sorry, but you see, his retardation is astronomic.'

Do looks his way.

And Bogard proceeds. 'The other day in World Orientation Class he asked: "Have I been to Europe?" Well, Sir, these days, business trips and kids parties go into space! The kids laugh at him, and they're only five or six year old themselves...'

The chart is consulted.

'Perhaps,' Rich explores, 'it's a little early for *World Orientation?*'

'In playful projects, mind! They stimulate independence, but your s... Excuse me, Doneus doesn't know where to start.'

'Sorry, doctor, could it be possible that he would fit in a class where the teacher is more... Present? Or supportive?'

'Mr Beaumond, listen to this question: if you were the father, would you put him in shackles? That wouldn't have any effects on Doneus. Do you know what he does at lunchtime? Or bunk-off time!' Magnanimously Bogard is trying to hide his indignation. 'He makes for the Sanatorium down the road, climbs the wall that's even too high for my eyes, should I wish to see, picks the lovely lilacs and offers them to the convalescents with plaids over their legs in deck chairs on the porch or veranda!'

Do gives him a sad smile.

'But how can you tell...' Rich tries.

'Well, Sir, I can tell that this is no *small* brain flaw. If we had more on his background, there might have been time for a remedy of some kind. Was it a complex birth or pregnancy? I mean, sorry, is this little person left in the lurch? Can a child carry such a *secret?*'

While the whole room has been still from concentration, Rich asks: 'If that issue is resolved, could there be a recovery or remedy?'

'Not in my school, I'm afraid. His social isolation would be fatal.'

'Excuse me, doctor, you have *created* it!'

'Or, Mr Beaumond, would you prefer a brain test? It's merely diagnostic procedure: they lift the brainpan and connect electrodes, which provide all information.'

Just when everybody is giving up – 'For heaven's sake, put him in Very Special Education Indeed!' – Helen is helped by an insane coincidence that can be nothing but fate and touching destination.

At a *given* moment Do asks Rich: 'Can I call you Dad?'

Rich has bought a football, installed swings, and now he's building a warehouse with cranes and lifts; this personal design may be based on a dolls house, but with a foundation of love.

They go cycling around a landscape where time is quiet, past willows and reeds by creeks and meres, to a farm with animals in fields.

On the way back they stop in a cosy restaurant, and after a stack of pancakes Do says: 'I'm fulfilled up.'

Man & animal's disjointed self-esteem

How grateful we are for claws and jaws,
to fight and defend, while mister wisdom
can move his head three hundred degrees!
Well, the very idea has fatigued me already:
what view of the world will ensue from that?

The Decathlon is hot, stadium stands are crammed, the IAAF build new arenas and young athletes find big rich sponsors, except those at universities; they run and jump their legs off to win contract renewals.

There's no more jogging or skating going on in the parks. It's all starting blocks and pole vaults and hurdles now – can't get around them. As the shot-put is boundless, injuries confront Health Departments until global Health Care is established in which America does participate.

In order to finance that, American millionaires will pay fair taxes too.

One of the first highlights of the summer season has begun: the WELSO weekend in Birmingham, preceded by a gala where the Ferrari is on show: a bonus for the winner, provided by a surviving bank. At the right moment, athletes from Uganda have arranged some transfers to European countries, where the Ferrari will come out better too.

For seven hours a day a Swiss runner has prepared himself in a low-pressure tunnel, and by the time the Major begins in Mexico, he'll switch to the high-pressure tunnel.

'Are you looking forward to the prospect?' a journalist asks during the gala, and more young athletes rapidly climbing the ranks feel involved. Foster Parents and Playgirl get massive response for an all-star action on ITV4.

The audience can't wait, they phone-film and watch themselves on the ultra screens.

'Hi, Mum! Can you see me waving? Don't you love my design specs? Plain glass is the latest rage.'

Jim's 100m and shot-put are a slight come-down, so that at least *some* competition is on, but with the jumping events all sovereignty is restored, and after the 400m on the first day's night, he's beyond reach again.

The wind has dropped and the lights are on in the fresh and fragrant air. The stands have grown placid. Gathering their gear, the Decathletes have time for a relaxing yawn... when Jim finds a packet of weed and suddenly realizes what WELSO means. The arena is green and yellow with WELSO boarding, which does give a tasteful and characteristic atmosphere.

'Is the Main Sponsor a weed company?' he asks Jenkins, the tournament director from Harvard.

'Sure, and you've done a helluva job! Look, how many do you think are smoking in the stands?'

Jim waits and collects himself, presses the REC key of a machine on the desk and asks: 'Excuse me?'

'... ... but I'm sorry, Mr. Beaumond, I didn't mean to...'

After Jenkins' tentative explanation, Jim leaves the room as well as the tournament while Jenkins calls out: 'You can't do this, we'll sue you!'

'I'm doing it now.'

Most of the crowd head off during the javelin event on the second day, not for ethical reasons of principle but out of boredom, because compared to Jimmy's natural light-footedness the rest of the field are a cumbersome bunch in shock, now that they get a chance to win something for once.

The fine for Jim's breach of contract is considerable, if only a trifle of the tournament losses. Jenkins would be better off breaking with WELSO; removing the boarding overnight would have been less chaotic than what's occurring now. Nobody sees who wins! The photographers are in the hospital around people with javelin wounds.

And that is what Romy can be so happy about: her safety and peace make up for the past and present desolation. In an idyllic little cottage, rented for her by the Ransom House publisher, she stumbles upon television reports but quickly switches to the view outside, where no bodyguards or mobs or reporters are fighting. She feels vulnerable and perceptive with a retro-active effect.

Wearing casual and natural clothes, with Nordic socks in slippers, Romy nestles on the soft sofa by the window, where the light is mild on her skin. Through the panes in wooden frames a squirrel peeks in among birds and butterflies and lots of new leaves. Her eyes roam back inside along the wild flowers in potters' vases, the rocking chair on a woollen rug, hot chocolate and buttered ginger cake.

Lost in thought, she sips and takes little bites.

The minute she's grown more conscious again of what's behind her in life, she takes her pretty thick writing pad and elegant fountain pen, puts a tin of liquorice next to her, settles in the cushions and listens to the rustling in the garden, and writes, not as fast as Barbara Cartland but word for word without a lie.

She would be completely happy here in the remote cabin, if it weren't for the knowledge that her book is nearing its final stage. Will she give it a riveting ending with a hint of hope? Something clear and pleasing to the multitude? Or can titillating subtlety stand out in the glutted market?

A sharp or open ending would be bad for the film producer, and none of the handsome advance is based on that sort of mood.

What can she really decide?

Her unspoilt singing during the writing spells escapes the public notice and the singing itself is one of the few things from her Wise-Girls life that she does miss. Her voice is truly strong. Will she transform or sublimate loneliness for closure?

For a while all the internet pictures of her little half brother at school pass her by:
- working hard in a corner
- sunk in melancholy
- pushed around by other kids

- chewing on a pen, alone in a room
- by himself in a hall
- painting a bloody good mural
- sadly upset, not understanding the anger of cleaners

child and source

the openness connects without strings
what it's made of to who moves it along
to the delicate limits, where no end begins

Helen doesn't need to think of a solution for Do anymore; it's put into her mouth – if awkwardly – and Do walks over to her. In reality shows this is all very new, original, and ground-breaking: when they sit on the sofa next to each other, the camera reclines poetically, slowly, out through a window and further, just catching the bird that lands on the sill as if it knows that some support may be needed here.

Helen talks, explains and cries.

In the sky a plane goes by, silvery against the deep blue in the sunshine.

Correspondingly Do's eyes are wide open and innocent, watching the Helen who tries and still cries.

He looks and listens attentively until her face is getting rather smudged, then he says: 'Don't do Botox.'

Helen fears that it's his phase of denial, but he asks: 'Can I see this bio dad?'

Which makes her resolute or reckless. 'I'll do my best.'

'Now?'

'No, my Do, you're off to school.'

'But my belly aches.'

'I can imagine. From nerves?'

'What's that?'

'Like being terribly curious and excited?'

'Yes.'

'Alright,' Helen says, 'I'll phone school and a few people far away, and you can record any questions for your birth dad. Press PAUSE when you want to think.'

'Don't need to.'

'Oh. Alright. See you soon.'

And she leaves him in full faith.

'Who are you? How old are you? I'm glad if you know me... Are you hoping that we don't live far away? Do you know Mum? Can I come over? Do you speak English? I'm learning it, but Miss Paula says I don't. Are you dumb too? Will you come over? What kind of bike have you got? If a bomb drops, can you hide? Not in the attic! Are you good at computers or Monopoly? Nobody wants to play it with me, but I *can*. Have you got a diploma? I'm going to watch Jimmy, back in a minute!'

In the drowsy heat of South America, at some altitude among exotic trees, Jim is floating over almost six meters of pole vault, evoking terrific slow-motion pictures. He turns and descends and lands lightly on the cushion, to spring around dance-like. The whole stadium is cheering in abundant sunlight.

The athletes have long afternoon breaks in cool rooms, except the decathlon men, who break their limits for days of extremely varied efforts, unlike the ten-second sprint called *King's Event* in some languages.

In the field centre the big sprinkler is on and Jim runs and splashes, glides and sops, arms wide from rapture. The audience love this even more than a crash or the clash over a false start. Then he lies in the grass, building focus and pleasure for the next discipline of millimetre precision, filmed by ruthless hyper-zoom lenses.

The Sponsor is a company of *Super-abSorbent Sani's*. Sadly the monthly discomfort is just as natural as tobacco and weed, which grow in the open of their own accord, and half the crowd are female, zooming in on the full-body and supple muscle motion, still it's taking some getting used to that the logo on the training suits is a panty liner.

Soon Do is talking into the recorder again: 'Are you afraid to touch a slug? How big are you? How far can you jump? Have you got a dad? Can you sing good songs? My favourite was The Wise Girls, but now it's Alli's music. Can you play the cello? I'm not going to bed. Or will you read to me? I always get cold milk. I'm thirsty!'

Along with the runners, the whole arena is breathless. It's a famous danger of the 1500 meters: you can *taste* fulfilment before it's there. Fatigue is getting to you mentally: you envy people who sit and drink, chew and sleep; what you need so badly. Each part of the body is mad from pain, unless you can ignore all that and feel no fear, so you're free to move around a space where satisfaction has waited for ages, growing from the tailbone to the crone until it's autonomous, the way you get shivers or goose bumps.

Jim counts no laps and sees no screen or rail cam, he feels the wind like loving lips. Other runners already spread and lag; he's alone with himself and his breathing, reaching boundaries that need to be crossed, while the body is merely an instrument.

Now there's a hush of awe. The crowd forget to watch themselves or the lap scores. Not until their hero lies on the grass with jelly legs, do they see his finishing time. What the hell has he done? After nine events he was so far ahead, he would have won doing a stroll or a dance.

The paramedics bring oxygen and a stretcher, but he whispers: 'Let me be,' so quietly that they listen.

Jim smells the delicate evening dew, feels the earth beneath and hears birds behind all the voices, twittering: 'Is this a World Record or a Personal Best?'

When the senses in his legs return, he groans from the toes upwards, opens his eyes and drinks water slowly, spreads the fingers and rolls a bit, heaving his lungs out, leaning on hands and knees.

It's a while before he crawls up and brushes tears away.

Some bystanders laugh, others cry out and applaud. Officials lay a hand on his back, technicians fidget with equipment, a commentator swallows, and all is replayed in zooms and slower motion to classic music, till he walks again, if shying from tough hugs.

The Network director suspects that something is going unnoticed. In the Commercial Rooms phones are screaming when breaks are skipped or omitted.

At last Jim stumbles into the Interview Room and dutifully answers these tremendous, meaningful, original questions again. 'Where the heck do you get it from: spooky sponsors?'

'Well, it's no secret.'

'So you've shattered the World Record, and how do you feel?'

'Wonderful, if tired.'

'Can you *describe* that?'

Jim takes this interest seriously. 'You know, millions of people are in need.'

'Why?'

'They don't have television.'

'Will you be a new Milo of Kroton?'

'But I've just become Jimmy Beaumond...'

'And do you think in terms of body, soul or mind?'

'Well... All three?'

'What about the other holy trinity?'

'Not sure what...'

'Then what do you believe or know for sure?'

'Sorry, I can't really think anymore.'

'And if you *feel*?'

'Oh um, the chakras and aura.'

For a spell they're speechless, but then comes a question of extra importance: 'Do you wax or shave your chest and more?'

'Of course, for mammoth cameras and worldwide television.'

'And for a hundredth or a thousandth of a second?'

'Yeah, so much weight.'

'Like the difference between Olympic silver and gold?'

'Yes, life-defining.'

'So do you seek the balance between Tension and De-tension?'

'Hm, difficult.'

'Between Urge and Control?'

Jim nods hard. 'Yes!'

And nobody detects anything threatening.

Reporter 10: 'What sports do you watch yourself?'

'The bloopers, of course, with juicy crashes, and Tractor Pulling, Desert Racing, Water Scooting and Motor Climbing.'

'Why?'

'Because these noble and classic sports fit into the unspoilt landscape so... soundlessly and athletically.'

'So should they be Olympic events?'

'Definitely.'

'Then why are the Committees being so fussy?'

'Well, if the Olympics were originally a spiritual or brotherly preparation for war...'

'Anything left for you to *learn*?'

'Um, peace and patience.'

'Oh. Between the hurdles?'

'And,' Jim is grinding his teeth, 'at the start or finish.'

'What does this *mean* to you?'

'The crown of my life.'

'Ha! The *finishing* touch!'

Reporter 22: 'What was going on in your mind?'

'Nothing, actually, to my own surprise.'

'And during the National Anthem?'

'Oh, absolutely.'

There's a silence and the tension of pleasure heightens, while Jim is turning grey in the face.

Then: 'You were crying, weren't you? From pain or grief? Or maybe relief of some kind?'

The press mob gets louder and louder again, fighting for space among ample cam flashing. Some equipment is broken, but Jim is motionless. Between questions there's no time for answers; he's not even trying anymore. And sometimes there's almost sympathy: 'What do your *family* think of all this? Are you going on a holiday now? Well-deserved! Where to?'

Modestly in the back, with a bad view of what's going on, an elderly man tries to make use of a lull: 'Your low grip on the pole, with the jump in the centre of the bar, does that require a sp...'

It would be an interesting technical question, but a late colleague who had to finish a piece on Prince Reginald's divorce first, beats him to it: 'Is your fiancée around?'

This press meet is *live* on television, a source of inspiration and solace to those who struggle with life because their sport is no job, while the body can train eight hours a day without ending up in a black hole. At least people talk about it now: 'Life after medals.'

Touched and full of empathy, many a Beaumond friend has tuned in, including the lawyers and counsellors, Benedict and Bogard, Do's teachers and therapists, the Confusion Group, consultant Fisher, manager Donald, Roy Milton, and Bummy in a satellite café.

Nearly,
for no reason
or so it may seem,
along massive clouds…

Hey, that swerving little bird
can't believe it's happening either.

If you have a mind for feeling,
please know what I mean.

Quieter, more reflective, Do has new questions and thoughts: 'Are you scared of darkness or spiders? Can you run fast and not fall? Are you cold at night? I wet my bed and Mum is sad. Do you ever have a broken leg? I got stabbed by a gnat and my heart is hurt.'

And Jim has a difficult conversation with the IAAF Board, who are sorry to decline his petition for dispensation from the press obligations.

In tasteful grey and immaculate suits, the committee are seated in a row on one side of a large and shining conference table, all facing Jim gravely in his warm-coloured sport clothes. As they're in front of a big window, he sees only the as dark and vague shapes in counter-light.

'Sorry, I can't do the interviews anymore.'

'Why is that?'

'One more of those questions would finish me. I'm simply not up to their level.'

'Beaumond, you are unequalled!'

'No, I'm strangled by their intelligence.'

'Do you realize what the consequences would be?'

'Suspension for life, I guess.'

'Correct. So think a minute, please, because as the celebrated, international decathlete, you have a magnificent gift: the charisma of a diplomat and flaming orator! As the ultimate representative of Strength, Timing and Speed, you have the option, indeed, the *mission* to propagate.'

'What?'

'Let the *heart* speak. You've got it in you, for Peace & Economy.'

'Yes, Jim, open gates and work on fate.'

'*Break* fate!'

'Make a global statement for the nation.'

'You've got what it takes, don't waste it.'

'Waste *what*, Sir?'

'The basic nation's pride! Kill prejudice and hatred.'

Jim sighs a load of air out. What opportunities is he missing? How important is it for him to persevere? 'Sorry, you mean *Business*, and I'm no Missionary.'

'Ah, people do *listen* to you, Jimmy; stick to the essence of sports, be yourself, do what brings joy to your life, show them Beauty, Power and Peace – your deep strength! You can't keep it all to yourself, can you?'

In the full universe Dono is a world of his own: 'Are you good at mowing? I can help Rich. Have you ever stinged a wasp? I spit the pips out of an apple. Can you spit far and climb high? Ouch, I'm biting my teeth. Do you cry a lot? When you fall, you must jump on your feet. I cry only if it's not fair because she promised! Will you send a photo then or have you got a boy already? I'm not tired, but...'

While Jim is on his way to Alli, to share his decision with her, Helen has gone to the extremes of her doings, and she traces Do's bio dad.

His name is Norman and his willingness dazzles her, so that doubts are striking again: this can't be good, can it? But soon she discovers why.

Norm is twenty and the cause of his young donorship lies in his youth as well. As a prodigy – and she wonders: why is that word hiding in 'Prodigal Son'? – he's bullied; he leaves one school after the other and falls into the hands of a paediatrician. With a medical balls test (Norm's testicles in one hand and wooden measure beads in the other) this kind-hearted man finds that

Norm is likely to stay rather small, which becomes a tragedy because his parents are opposed to growth hormones.

The mental consequence may be repaired in a major way: reassert yourself vigorously via the cause of your grief.

His virility is enormous and a sort of self-esteem can compensate other matters. The photographer and designer of the Sperm Spa donor catalogue are magicians: it's just as if Norm's portrait renders his *inner* measures. In a Freudian or spiritual or dyslexic manner, a few little errors of great significance and chance occur when details like stature and width are filled out.

'Can Do Skype or send chat-mails?' Helen suggests on the intercontinental line, quickly adding: 'No pictures for now, if you wish. He's not very good at writing yet, but he's got heaps to say.'

'OK.'

And Helen doesn't know to what extent the spontaneous digital contact needs interpretation or translation and omission.

'Have you ever had blood? I need an operation, says the doctor. In my head. Will you come over then or are you scared of clinics? I lost my tooth. Do you have holidays?'

'I do,' Norm types, 'but um...'

'It's for your son!' Helen interferes personally. 'He's being expelled from school already because they don't understand him. It's only a couple of hours flying and in your parts it's much earlier.'

Neither logic nor humour comes across, and she goes on: 'Help us, Norm, it's Absolutely Fabulous here! You'll be a nice Uncle too, I mean, Romy and Jim are your age, and...' She throws a pleading look at Rich, who nods big-heartedly. '...there will be a cool bike for you, to go and see all the sights!'

Couldn't know better

Travelling just in case
(none of us is too able),
we keep changing planes.

More airports with stairs?

By chance we glance around,
having trouble reading the sign,
and suddenly believe: we are here.

Even before the cheap flight, people are staring as if a lost celebrity is on board. Crept away by a window is a young man called Norman, whose prominent glasses are very much like the pair of Do's headmaster, Benedict.

The 6-pm departure was delayed due to a severe storm, hanging there like a cosmic tumour, turning into a cloud burst that wipes the dust off trees and windows.

We can see and breathe again.

The leaves have a lovely sheen and scent.

All things heavy seem light, so finally the plane takes off, to pierce clusters of clouds now compact, then shredded in permanent motion. The sun has fought the wind and withdraws to set behind the ocean.

After the delay, dinner isn't served until ten, and owing to the time difference, breakfast follows presently. The sun that left the world – upset – a moment ago, is the picture of peace again.

Many people keep gazing at Norm, because *his* eyes have clearly not been lasered yet, and he seems to be memorizing a little dictionary. Nervously in a corner he cleans his glasses repeatedly and mumbles phrases half out loud, learning them with his eyes shut tight and the head back, like a high-school kid revising.

Now he heaves a sigh and checks his watch, then peers out the window at the violet sky, resting his hands on the book, prepared to land.

Thus Norm arrives on a morning without night.

Equally excited, Do and Helen are meeting him at the airport. They give him a hand, a kiss and hug. His remarkable glasses almost fall off.

On the way home Helen has to concentrate on driving, but Do can point to the scenery and say the English words: 'Cow, mill, electripole,' which Norm is repeating so comically that they have a hearty laugh. Stunningly fast he's learning a whole new language!

At about the same time, Romy gets up, stretches in full satisfaction and walks out into the serene country stillness with bird songs and rabbit hops. She's cherishing the warmth, taking deep and slow breaths. Profoundly content, she sits down on a tree trunk.

Richard and Norman are heart-meltingly shy while Helen beams with pride. Rich is a wonderful host; he's baked a cake, made coffee with freshly grinded beans, pouring and offering timidly. He also helps translating as far as necessary, and his emotions are repressed when Helen tells Norm: 'This is your boy.'

'From the plane,' Do asks, 'could you see the good view?'

Norm wipes his eyes, groping for words with a charming accent. 'En...thralling. You fly with me on a day?'

'Yes. And you play ball with me? I've practised a hundred times, so don't think I'm a wimp.'

'No, yes.'

'Are you staying over?'

Norm blinks gratefully.

'Have you got pyjamas?'

'Sure, is it cold here?'

'Do you want hot coco?'

As Norm rubs his tired eyes again, Do gets the glasses and puts them on most naturally, as if pushed or drawn and driven. 'Wow, nice, look!'

'Oh, thanks, but I'm not...'

'Mum looks good too!' Do says maturely.

'Well, darling,' Helen begins, 'I don't think...'

'And Rich... Hey, the cupboards are straight. The room is all still, and so big.'

Do moves around and reels a bit, but soon he's avoiding furniture in perfect balance, which did improve already after Joy's programme. 'We can look *out*.'

He stops in front of the bookcase and reads nearly fluently: 'Lord of the Flies, Portrait of the Artist as a Young Man, The Bible, The Child in Time.'

Then he types an equation on the computer.

'What kind of glasses are those?' Helen mutters childishly.

And Norm does understand. 'Corrism.'

'Charisma?'

'No, short for Prism and Correction.'

'Sorry, for a sec you had me think Prison, silly simple me. So, correcting what, if I may ask?'

'Well, muscles in my eyes do not work. Bad nerve bundles. One looks here and the other so stupid. Eyes must be crosswise to the brain; if they don't co ordinate, it gets hopeless. No correlation.'

'Must be genetic!'

'On whose side?' Rich mumbles to himself.

'No link between the two brain halves,' Norm continues modestly and slowly, 'even if each is a genius. It's classic medical. In some big language, the word brain is still plural, by example *hersens*.'

'I've known it all along!' Helen acknowledges. 'Just like China, right? Our country is so dumb!'

'So,' Rich checks, waving his arm around, 'Do did always perceive this, as it were, but he never realized it, so to speak, because details were lost, basically, between the eyes and brain?'

'Yes, no nerve connection.'

Helen cries to Do: 'Careful with those glasses!'

And Norm adds: 'No complement means no recognition, so no information.'

Some of this has been translated, but it's the very words of Latin origin that Norm knows best, since they recur in a lot of languages, Anglo Saxon or Germanic.

Helen is gasping. 'Tell me now, Do: what's twenty minus five?'

'No,' Rich intervenes, 'he needs to *see* and process that first.'

'Ah, yes, and then?'

'In the second instance he'll learn how it works,' Rich explains patiently. 'His brain will pick things up and remember, until they're automatised, right?'

'Internalised,' Norm corrects humbly.

There are no words for it,
unless they're trying to tell
that *misunderstood* won't do.

Sentences tend to get shorter
(without ending or beginning)
but they might send a message
to a speaker who remained silent.

In the far perspective of a disbeliever:
can vision be such that a mist is full of it?

Norm stays and lends his glasses to Do as often as possible, until
a pair of his own can be ordered.

'What a strong move of fate!' Helen tells Do. 'It can't be
coincidence, can it, that you were ill before the holidays, or else
you'd be at that VSE School now. So horrid and insulting for the
kids there, that it seems to stand for Very *Stupid* Education instead
of *Special*. What were they thinking! With just one brain half?'

And Rich mourns: 'It's a pointless cliché, but if only we'd
know before.'

'Yeah,' Helen exclaims, 'life can be so cruel! Some people have
all the bad luck.'

'Would that be random?'

'No! Don't think like that, because if this had been different,
we'd never have met Norm.'

The doorbell rings.

It's Headmaster Benedict, whose glasses are similar to Norm's,
and before anyone can fill him in on current developments, he
makes for Do and gives him a parcel, which Do unwraps calmly.
It's a big plastic cube, the size of a football, with the numbers one
to six, and a card saying: Dice of Life.

'Hello, Do,' Benedict says, 'we're so sorry that you have to go!
From the whole school, this is a farewell gift. Hey, are you wearing
Corrism glasses? Had them since I was two, when people called
me retarded! After migraines and madness and loneliness, we

found this eye-doctor who corrected my prism. He didn't care if it was called *un*scientific. Poor boy, if only you'd *told* me! So modest, this pioneering eye specialist; he hated publicity. I did press him and said: "*Share* your knowledge! *Tell* the world about your invention." You see, I'm so for openness – do communicate in any way!'

Do's eyes are large and wide.

Benedict sighs. 'The shy man just said: "I've been at all the institutes and universities, I've written articles and *shown* and *proven*, but even if they see it with their own eyes, they can't believe it."'

Helen thunders up to him and grabs his glasses, to put them on for a sec herself. She takes a close and steaming look at the man and staggers back with a scream. 'I can see no future for you!'

Benedict is gazing in a daze, retaining a minimum of dignity, and Helen hands the glasses to Do, who returns the others to Norm, puts Benedict's pair on and is deeply pleased.

'What are you doing?' the headmaster stammers.

'Up your glass!' Do says in an authentic accent.

Inward bound

He went on shuffling
when there was a hush
and eyes prevented him.

Aching to be united,
he couldn't think how,
but some kids are found.

All around the pitch, a big stadium is roaring, but suddenly there's
a silence when Do appears on the far end, focused and confident.
He takes the *Dice of Life* and puts it at his feet, the way it's placed
on the penalty mark. Unstoppable, to sublime rhythmical music,
he starts dribbling and pushing it and running at top speed,
playing it with glorious moves and passionate manoeuvres, the
deftest of dodges, blinding instead of blindly, to pass Benedict
and Bogard and assistant, the remedial teacher, a dozen regular
teachers, all former classmates and more, going for the deciding
goal.

Out Now:
Women Writing the Weird
Edited by Deb Hoag

WEIRD

1.	Eldritch: suggesting the operation of supernatural influences; "an eldritch screech"; "the three weird sisters"; "stumps . . . had uncanny shapes as of monstrous creatures" —John Galsworthy; "an unearthly light"; "he could hear the unearthly scream of some curlew piercing the din" —Henry Kingsley

2.	Wyrd: fate personified; any one of the three Weird Sisters

3.	Strikingly odd or unusual; "some trick of the moonlight; some weird effect of shadow" —Bram Stoker

WEIRD FICTION

1.	Stories that delight, surprise, that hang about the dusky edges of 'mainstream' fiction with characters, settings, plots that abandon the normal and mundane and explore new ideas, themes and ways of being. —Deb Hoag

RRP: £14.99 ($28.95).

featuring

Nancy A. Collins, Eugie Foster, Janice Lee, Rachel Kendall, Candy Caradoc, Mysty Unger, Roberta Lawson, Sara Genge, Gina Ranalli, Deb Hoag, C. M. Vernon, Aliette de Bodard, Caroline M. Yoachim, Flavia Testa, Aimee C. Amodio, Ann Hagman Cardinal, Rachel Turner, Wendy Jane Muzlanova, Katie Coyle, Helen Burke, Janis Butler Holm, J.S. Breukelaar, Carol Novack, Tantra Bensko, Nancy DiMauro, and Moira McPartlin.

Out Now:
Bite Me, Robot Boy
Edited by Adam Lowe

Bite Me, Robot Boy is a seminal new anthology of poetry and fiction that showcases what Dog Horn Publishing does best: writing that takes risks, crosses boundaries and challenges expectations. From Oz Hardwick's hard-hitting experimental poetry, to Robert Lamb's colourful pulpy science fiction, this is an anthology of incandescent writing from some of the world's best emerging talent.

Featuring
S.R. Dantzler, Oz Hardwick, Maximilian T. Hawker, Emma Hopkins, A.J. Kirby, Stephanie Elizabeth Knipe, Robert Lamb, Poppy Farr, Wendy Jane Muzlanova, Cris O'Connor, Mark Wagstaff, Fiona Ritchie Walker and KC Wilder.

Out Now:
Cabala
Edited by Adam Lowe

From gothic fairytale to humorous pop-culture satire, five of the North's top writers showcase the diversity of British talent that exists outside the country's capital and put their strange, funny, mythical landscapes firmly on the literary map.

Over the course of ten weeks, Adam Lowe worked with five budding writers as part of the Dog Horn Masterclass series. This anthology collects together the best work produced both as a result of the masterclasses and beyond.

Featuring
Jodie Daber, Richard Evans, Jacqueline Houghton, Rachel Kendall and A.J. Kirby

Out Now:
Nitrospective
Andrew Hook

Japanese school children grow giant frogs, a superhero grapples with her secret identity, onions foretell global disasters and an undercover agent is ambivalent as to which side he works for and why. Relationships form and crumble with the slightest of nudges. World catastrophe is imminent; alien invasion blase. These twenty slipstream stories from acclaimed author Andrew Hook examine identity and our fragile existence, skid skewed realities and scratch the surface of our world, revealing another—not altogether dissimilar—layer beneath.

Nitrospective is Andrew Hook's fourth collection of short fiction.

RRP: £12.99 ($22.95).

Acclaim for the Author

"Andrew Hook is a wonderfully original writer" —Graham Joyce

"His stories range from the darkly apocalyptic to the hopefully visionary, some brilliant and none less than satisfactory"
—*The Harrow*

"Refreshingly original, uncompromisingly provocative, and daringly intelligent" —*The Future Fire*

ND - #0510 - 270225 - C0 - 229/152/12 - PB - 9781907133725 - Gloss Lamination